Tiny Tales from India

Tiny Tales from India

A Book of Two Hundred 100-Word Stories

Laura Gibbs

Contents

About This Book

This book opens with traditional folktales from the Panchatantra, the Hitopadesha, and the Katha-Sarit-Sagara ("Story-Stream-Ocean"), plus Jataka tales of the Buddha's past lives. You will also find stories of the Indian gods and goddesses, plus parables from Ramakrishna, who was both a sadhu (holy man) and storyteller. The book closes with anecdotes about the legendary jesters Tenalirama from the court of Krishnadevaraya in southern India and Birbal from the court of Akbar in the north. The two hundred stories in this book represent only a tiny fraction of the Indian storytelling tradition. To read more stories from India, visit: **India.LauraGibbs.net**

The paragraph you just read about this book is exactly one hundred words long, as is this paragraph, and that's also the length of each story in this book. The stories go fast, but you can slow down when you find one you like. Read it again. Let it sink in. Maybe even write your own version of the story, using your imagination to add more details.

Meanwhile, if you don't like a story, don't get bogged down; just move on to the next one. There are more 100-word stories from India, plus stories from other cultural traditions, at:

100Words.LauraGibbs.net

The Stories

1. THE LION AND THE RABBIT

Every day, the lion demanded that the animals send him a victim to eat.

One day, it was the rabbit's turn. The rabbit took his time on the way, thinking of a plan to escape the lion.

"Why are you late?" the lion roared.

"My apologies," said the rabbit. "I saw an even bigger lion, and I was frightened."

"Show me!" the lion commanded.

The rabbit took the lion to a well. "The lion's in there," said the rabbit.

The lion looked in and saw the other lion. Infuriated, he jumped in the well and drowned, attacking his own reflection.

2. THE LION-KING AND THE CAMEL

The lion-king was starving.

"You must eat the royal camel," the crow advised.

"But he's my devoted courtier!" the lion protested.

"Don't worry," said the jackal.

"He'll agree!" said the leopard.

So the lion-king summoned his courtiers. "I'm starving!" he roared.

"Eat me!" said the crow.

"You're just skin and feathers," the jackal scoffed. "Eat me!"

"You're too scrawny," observed the leopard. "Eat me!"

This show of loyalty inspired the camel, who assumed that another courtier would speak up to save his life also. "The leopard's meat is tough," the camel exclaimed. "Eat me!"

So the lion ate the camel.

3. THE LION-KING AND THE JACKAL

The lion-king had grown old. "Fetch me something easy to kill!" he said to the jackal, his minister.

The jackal found a she-donkey in a dusty stable.

"I'll take you to a pasture of fresh green grass!" he said.

The donkey followed the jackal eagerly straight to the lion, but he was too weak; when the lion lunged for her, she escaped.

"Come back!" said the jackal. "The lion loves you! He wants to make you his queen."

"Me? Queen?"

The foolish donkey followed the jackal again. This time, the lion killed her. "Delicious!" he exclaimed, and the jackal agreed.

4. A STORY FOR THE LION-KING

"Tell me a story that goes on forever," the lion king shouted, "or you will all die."

"You're the best storyteller," the animals said to the jackal. "Please save us!"

The jackal smiled and began. "O King, a fisherman went fishing with his net."

"What next?" asked the lion.

"He caught many fish, but the net was torn, and a fish escaped."

"What next?"

"A second fish escaped."

"What next?"

"A third fish escaped."

The lion yawned.

"And a fourth. A fifth… A sixth…"

The lion fell asleep listening to the endless story, and so the jackal saved the animals.

5. THE LION AND THE CAT

A lion lived in a cave where there was a mouse who kept nibbling his mane, so the lion decided to hire a cat.

"I'll pay you to defend me from that mouse!" he promised.

The cat prowled the cave, and the terrified mouse stayed hidden in its hole.

The happy lion shared his food with the cat, and she had never eaten so well!

Finally, though, the mouse had to come out to look for food, whereupon the cat caught the mouse and killed it.

Then the lion stopped feeding the cat, and she died of hunger, poor thing.

6. THE LION IN THE JACKAL'S CAVE

A hungry lion hid inside a cave. "I'll eat whoever comes in," he thought to himself.

The lion waited there all day.

The jackal who lived in that cave finally came home and said, "Hello, Cave!"

The lion said nothing.

"Cave, you know you're supposed to answer!" said the jackal.

The lion was uncertain what to do. "Hello to you!" the lion roared, and the cave made his roar sound even louder.

The jackal laughed as he ran away. "You foolish lion!" he shouted. "That's how I know whether the cave is safe or not. Next time, remember: keep quiet."

7. THE BLUE JACKAL

There was once a jackal who fell into a vat of blue indigo dye. The other animals were amazed when they saw the blue jackal!

"The gods have sent me to be your ruler," the blue jackal explained. He made the lion his prime minister, the tiger was the royal treasurer, and the elephant was his doorkeeper.

One day, though, the blue jackal heard other jackals howling in the distance. He could not resist; he began howling too.

"He's just an ordinary jackal!" shouted the other animals.

So the lion and the tiger attacked their former king and killed him.

8. THE JACKAL AND HIS BROTHERS

A lioness had given birth to twins.

The lion went hunting and caught a baby jackal. "Eat this!" he told her.

The lioness, however, nursed the jackal, who grew up with the lions.

One day the cubs saw an elephant; the lions wanted to attack, but the jackal warned them away.

"It's too dangerous!" he said.

The lion twins snarled. "You're such a coward!"

The lioness feared for the jackal. "You aren't really a lion," she told him. "You should run away before your lion brothers kill you."

So the jackal went away and found his jackal brothers at last.

9. THE TIGER CUB AND THE GOATS

A she-tiger died giving birth.

Wild goats found the cub and cared for him.

The cub ate grass like the goats, bleated like the goats, and thought he really was a goat.

A tiger then attacked the goats and found the cub. "Why are you eating grass? Why are you bleating?" he asked.

"That's what goats do," replied the cub.

"But you're a tiger!" he said.

Then he took the cub to a pond. "Look: that's your face! That's you!"

Thus the big tiger became a teacher to the cub who finally learned how to be a tiger after all.

10. THE LION AND THE RAM

A ram once strayed from its flock and wandered into the forest.

In the forest there lived a lion who had never seen a ram before.

So when the lion first saw this ram, he stared in amazement. "Look at those horns! That creature might be even more powerful than me!" he thought, and he carefully avoided the ram.

A few days later, though, he saw the ram again. It was eating grass.

"This creature is a grass-eater!" said the lion to himself. "It is surely no match for me."

The lion then sprang on the ram and killed it.

11. THE JACKAL AND THE DEAD ELEPHANT

A jackal found a dead elephant but couldn't chew through the elephant's tough hide.

Then a lion arrived.

Terrified, the jackal said, "I saved the elephant for you!"

"I don't eat what others kill," said the lion. "You may have it."

The lion left, and a leopard arrived.

The jackal shouted, "Hurry! Let's eat the lion's elephant before he returns."

The leopard bit into the elephant, tearing the hide with her sharp teeth and claws.

Then the jackal shrieked, "The lion's coming!"

Fearing the lion, the leopard ran off, leaving the jackal to feast on the whole elephant by himself.

12. LION, JACKAL, AND CAMEL

The lion was starving, as were his attendants: a jackal and a camel.

The jackal proclaimed, "I dreamed that Yama, God of Death, will grant rebirth to the devoted courtier who offers his body as food."

Without hesitation, the camel declared, "I accept Yama's promise of rebirth!"

So the lion and the jackal killed the camel.

Then, in the distance, they heard the jingling bells of a camel caravan.

"It's Yama and his Death-Caravan coming to avenge the camel!" shouted the jackal. "Run away, O King, run away!"

The lion ran, and the jackal had the whole camel to himself.

13. THE JACKAL AND THE CROW

A crow perched high in a tree, eating some delicious fruit.

A jackal decided to flatter the crow, hoping she would drop the fruit so that he could catch it.

"Fair lady, you look like a peacock up there!" he said to the crow. "Your feathers are dazzling. I've never seen anyone as beautiful and as graceful as you!"

The crow then flattered the jackal in return. "Kind sir, you look like a handsome young tiger!" she said, and as she spoke, all the fruit fell out of her mouth.

The jackal then grabbed the fruit and ran away, laughing.

14. THE JACKAL AND THE PEACOCK

A jackal and a peacock were friends.

One day the peacock ate some plums, while the jackal ate a lamb.

The peacock then planted the plum-pits. "I'll grow some plums!"

The jackal planted the bones. "I'll grow some lambs!"

The plum-pits sprouted, but not the bones.

The peacock mocked the jackal. "Your crop is a failure," he said, laughing.

Then one day the jackal didn't catch anything for supper, and he thought about how the peacock had mocked him.

"If I can't have lamb," the jackal decided, "I can have peacock!"

So the jackal killed the peacock and ate him.

15. THE JACKAL AND THE OTTERS

There were once two otters who caught a fish, and then they quarreled about how to divide it.

"The middle is mine," one otter said. "You can have the head and the tail."

"No!" said the other otter. "I want the middle! I'll give you the head and the tail."

A greedy jackal came by. "I'll be glad to judge between you," he said.

The otters explained what had happened.

"Oh, that's easy!" the jackal exclaimed. "You take the head… and you take the tail…" and then the jackal ran away with the middle part of the fish for himself.

16. THE JACKAL AND THE RAMS

There was once a greedy jackal who was prowling around, looking for food.

He saw two angry rams fighting, running at each other and butting heads. The jackal noticed that each time the rams butted heads, blood dripped down on the ground.

"I bet that blood would be tasty!" thought the jackal.

So the jackal ran up and licked the blood off the ground.

"That is delicious," he thought. "I want to get every drop."

Foolish jackal! While he was licking the blood, the rams butted their heads together again, and the jackal was crushed to death between their horns.

17. THE JACKAL AND THE BULLOCK

A jackal once noticed the big balls that dangled from a bullock's behind, and they made his mouth water.

"What a delicious meal those would make!" the jackal thought. "And his balls are so heavy and so big. Surely they will fall down soon!"

So the jackal began following the bullock everywhere, waiting for the balls to fall down.

But they didn't fall down.

"Such big balls!" the jackal thought. "Why don't they fall down?"

Ever hopeful, he kept following the bullock.

Finally, though, he gave up.

"You can keep your balls!" he shouted. "They probably wouldn't taste good anyway."

18. THE JACKALS AND THE ELEPHANT

The jackals were stalking an especially large elephant, thinking that they could feast on him for days.

Finally the most cunning of the jackals went to the elephant and said, "O Great One, the animals met and elected you to be their king. I am to escort you to the coronation."

"I'm honored!" said the elephant happily.

The jackal then led the elephant into a swamp.

"Help!" shouted the elephant as he sank into the mud.

"Your courtiers are all coming to help you, Your Highness!" promised the jackal.

But the jackals did not help; instead, they devoured the elephant.

19. THE ELEPHANT AND THE SPARROW

A raging elephant knocked down a sparrow's nest, killing her chicks.

The mother vowed revenge.

"Help me, Woodpecker!" she said.

"Agreed," said Woodpecker. "Help us, Gnat!"

"Agreed," said Gnat. "Help us, Frog!"

"Agreed," said Frog.

Then Frog told them all what to do.

Gnat buzzed in the elephant's ear; the music made him shut his eyes.

Then Woodpecker stabbed the elephant's eyes so he wanted to jump in the water for relief.

Meanwhile, Frog croaked at the edge of a pit; the elephant ran towards the sound, thinking it was a pond, and he fell in the pit and died.

20. THE ELEPHANT-KING AND THE MICE

The elephant-king was a wise ruler who had a kind heart.

When he led his elephants through the fields, they crushed many mice under their big feet.

"Have mercy!" cried the mice, so the elephant-king ordered all the elephants to spare the mice by taking a different path.

Later, elephant-hunters came and caught some of the elephants in snares.

"Help us!" the elephants shouted, and the mice all came to their rescue, using their tiny teeth to chew through the ropes and free the elephants from the snares.

Thus the elephants learned that even small friends can be great friends.

21. THE ELEPHANTS AND THE RABBITS

There was a drought.

The elephant-herd searched for water and found a beautiful lake. When the elephants rushed to drink, they crushed many rabbits underfoot.

A brave rabbit spoke to the elephant-king as he drank. "I am the Moon's envoy!" proclaimed the rabbit. "The Moon says: you trampled my beloved rabbits."

"I'll ask forgiveness!" said the elephant-king, and he kneeled in the water.

The moon's reflection in the water shook violently.

"The Moon is even more angry!" said the rabbit. "Go away and never come back!"

The elephant-king, fearing the Moon's heavenly powers, departed, and the elephant-herd departed with him.

22. THE ELEPHANT AND THE MONKEY

An elephant and a monkey were boasting.

"I'm mighty!" said the elephant.

"I'm nimble!" said the monkey.

"But which of us is better?" asked the elephant.

"Let the owl judge!" said the monkey.

"I propose a test," said the owl. "Bring me mangos from across the river."

So they ran to the river, but the monkey couldn't cross.

"I'll carry you!" said the elephant.

They got to the mango tree, but the elephant couldn't reach the mangos.

"I'll fetch them!" said the monkey.

They brought the mangos to the owl who said, "Now you see: you two are better together!"

23. THE WEALTHY TOAD

A toad once happened to find a copper coin.

He grasped the coin in his mouth and carried it back to his hole.

"I am now a toad who possesses both wealth and power!" he thought to himself.

Then one day an elephant walked over the toad's hole.

The toad leaped forth, angrily shaking his foot at the departing elephant as if he were going to kick him.

"How dare you walk over my head!" he shouted. "I am a toad who possesses both wealth and power!"

Money can make you lose all sense of proportion, just like that toad.

24. THE BOASTFUL BEETLE

There was once a tiny beetle who one day wandered into a place where people had enjoyed a wild party the night before.

Seeing a puddle of liquor on the ground, the beetle started drinking, and soon he was drunk.

"I am so mighty," he yelled, "that the world cannot bear my weight!"

An elephant wandered by.

"I'm going to fight you, elephant!" the beetle boasted. "We'll see who is the most mighty!"

The elephant laughed as he pooped and peed on top of the beetle, killing the insect instantly.

The elephant then ran into the forest, trumpeting in triumph.

25. THE SELF-IMPORTANT INSECT

A farmer was walking through his fields one evening, headed home. The setting sun was a blazing ball of fire, while the rising moon glowed a brilliant silver.

"How glorious are the sun and the moon!" he exclaimed.

As he continued walking, he heard a tiny voice.

He stopped, looking for the source of the voice.

It was a firefly!

"They are cousins of mine, you know," said the firefly. "I am a creature of fiery light, just like my relatives, the sun and the moon."

The farmer laughed, amused at this tiny creature and its enormous sense of self-importance.

26. THE MONKEY AND THE FIREFLY

A monkey found a firefly.

The evening was cool, so the monkey said, "I'll warm myself by the light of this fire!"

At just that moment, a bird flew by, and she decided to enlighten the monkey. "That's not fire," the bird explained. "That's just a firefly."

The monkey ignored the bird, so she chirped more loudly. "That won't work: a firefly isn't the same as a fire!"

On and on she chattered, making the monkey more and more angry.

Finally, the monkey grabbed the bird and squashed her.

Moral of the story: Be careful when correcting someone else's errors.

27. THE MONKEY AND THE PEAS

A monkey high up in a tree saw some peas lying nearby on the ground.

He jumped down and gathered all the peas in his hands, and then went back up the tree to enjoy his feast.

"Delicious!" he said.

As he was eating, one of the peas fell out of his hand.

"Oh no!" he shouted.

He jumped down to grab the lost pea, and as he did, all the other peas fell out of his hands.

Hearing his shout, more monkeys came and started eating.

Because he couldn't let one pea go, the monkey lost all the rest.

28. THE CROCODILE AND THE MONKEY

Craving Monkey's heart for supper, Crocodile swam to the riverbank where Monkey lived.

"Let's go to Banana Island, Monkey!"

"But you know I can't swim."

"Don't worry! I'll carry you."

Greedy for bananas, Monkey jumped on.

Crocodile plunged deep under the water.

"What are you doing?" Monkey shrieked.

"I'm going to eat your heart for supper."

"But I left my heart in the tree!"

Monkey pointed to the fig tree on the riverbank.

"Well, go get it!" shouted Crocodile.

Crocodile swam back to shore, and Monkey leaped into the tree.

"You might fool me once," he cackled. "But only once!"

29. THE MONKEY AND THE ROCK

Crocodile noticed Monkey using a rock to cross the river, jumping from riverbank to rock, and then from rock to riverbank.

"I'll make my back look like a rock," thought Crocodile. "He'll jump on me, and I'll catch him!"

Monkey saw a suspicious new rock in the river, so before he jumped, Monkey said, "Hello, Rock!'

Crocodile said nothing.

Monkey shouted, "Hey, Rock! Why don't you answer me like you usually do?"

Crocodile realized he had to answer. "Hello, Monkey…" he said cautiously.

"Hello to you, Crocodile," Monkey cackled. "And goodbye! I won't be jumping on you today… or ever!"

30. THE CROW'S REVENGE

A snake raided a crow's nest and ate her chicks.

The crow vowed revenge.

She knew where the royal ladies bathed, leaving their jewelry beside the pool. The crow squawked loudly to make sure the queen saw her, and then she flew off with a golden necklace in her beak.

"Guards!" screamed the queen. "Go get my necklace!"

The crow then dropped the necklace in front of the snake's hole.

When the guards arrived, they saw the necklace and they saw the snake. They clubbed the snake to death and retrieved the necklace.

That's how the crow got her revenge!

31. THE CRAB'S ADVICE

There were two herons who lived in a tree, and at the foot of the tree was a snake.

One day, the snake ate the herons' chicks.

"We need help!" said the father heron.

"Let's ask the crab for advice," said the mother heron.

So they went to see the crab.

"You should scatter some fish from the mongoose hole to the snake hole," said the crab. "The mongoose will follow the fish and eat the snake!"

The herons did what the crab advised.

The mongoose ate the snake as they had hoped, but then it ate the herons too.

32. THE PARTRIDGE AND THE RABBIT

A partridge had a lovely home, but he left that home, temporarily, in search of food.

When he came back, he found a rabbit was living there.

"Get out of my home!" shouted the partridge.

"This is my home now!" the rabbit shouted back.

They went to a pious cat who lived by the Ganges to ask him to judge their case.

"My dear creatures," the cat said, "I am old and deaf. You must come closer... I still cannot hear you... Closer... That's better, just a little closer."

And then the cat ate the partridge and the rabbit too.

33. THE VULTURE AND THE CAT

A vulture, old and nearly blind, lived in a tree hollow.

The other birds pitied the vulture and fed him, and he looked after their chicks.

A cat approached the tree, but the vulture squawked, "No food for you here, cat!"

"I follow the spiritual path," replied the cat. "I no longer eat meat. I seek only to learn from elders like yourself."

Flattered, the vulture began preaching.

Meanwhile, the cat ate the chicks, carefully depositing their bones in the vulture's hollow.

The cat then left, and when the birds found the bones, they attacked the vulture and killed him.

34. THE HAWKS AND THE CROWS

The hawks and the crows agreed to go hunting together.

One day, they found a fox nearly dead of starvation.

"We'll eat the upper half of the fox," said the crows.

"And we'll eat the lower half," said the hawks.

The fox laughed. "I always thought hawks superior to crows. Surely the hawks, not the crows, deserve the upper half."

"Yes, we do!" shouted the hawks.

"No, you don't!" shouted the crows.

A great fight broke out, and the fox recovered her strength by feasting on the fallen birds.

Thus the weak can profit when the powerful quarrel amongst themselves.

35. THE JACKDAW AND THE GLOW-WORM

A jackdaw had caught a glow-worm and was about to eat her.

"Wait!" the insect said. "I know where you can get hundreds of glow-worms."

"Show me!" said the greedy bird. "Take me there now!"

The glow-worm took the jackdaw to a potter's workshop where there was a fire burning.

"See that light?" said the glow-worm. "Go eat those glow-worms there, and then I'll show you more."

The jackdaw ran up to the fire and tried to eat the sparks, but the fire burned his mouth... and when he went back to complain, the glow-worm had already made her escape.

36. THE BHARUNDA BIRD

Have you heard of the bharunda bird? This strange creature has two heads attached to a single body.

One day, a bharunda bird found a flower filled with nectar. The first head drank the nectar eagerly, and the nectar went into their shared stomach. "Delicious!" it said.

"Give me some!" shouted the other head.

"No!" shouted the first head. "I found it; I drink it!"

The second head was so angry that it found a poisonous fruit and ate it.

"Ha!" shouted the head. "That's my revenge."

The poisonous fruit went into their shared stomach, and the bharunda bird died.

37. THE HAWK AND THE FISH

A hawk had caught a fish.

Holding the fish in his talons, he rose up from the water, ready to fly home and enjoy his meal.

But crows suddenly swarmed all around him, a hundred or more, each one trying to snatch the fish.

The hawk flew up and he flew down… still the crows pursued him.

Left and right… the crows kept on chasing him.

Finally, the hawk let go of the fish.

The crows all flew off, chasing after the fish and leaving the hawk alone.

He settled on a branch and sighed thankfully, "At last, I'm free."

38. THE CROW AND THE SUNRISE

A foolish crow was convinced that his shrill caw-caw-caw caused the sun to rise each morning. Each day, he cawed in the darkness before dawn, knowing that the whole world depended on him to bring the sun.

One morning, however, the crow slept late.

He awoke to see the sun already high in the sky.

"Thank goodness another member of the crow family was awake this morning!" he thought to himself. "Otherwise, the earth might have spent the whole day in darkness."

This foolish crow shows us that the way you see yourself is a matter of opinion, not fact.

39. THE ANIMALS BOASTING

"My great valor makes me king of the jungle," roared the lion.

"But I am the most cunning of all," countered the fox.

"Just look at my feathers!" shrieked the peacock.

"Feathers are nothing compared to tusks!" trumpeted the elephant.

Meanwhile, a little toad croaked her own opinion:

"Lion, as king of the animals, you're a coveted trophy for hunters! Your fur, Fox, will be made into a coat. Humans will kill you for your feathers, Peacock, and they will kill you for your tusks, Elephant!"

"So I say," the toad concluded, "it's better to be small rather than mighty."

40. THE ANIMALS CHANGE PLACES

The animals and fish had gotten bored with their lifestyles and decided to switch places: the fish would live on the land, and the animals in the sea.

The result was a complete disaster.

As the fish came crawling over the land, eagles and hawks swooped down and devoured them.

The animals, meanwhile, couldn't breathe underwater, and most of them couldn't even swim, and thus they died in the sea.

"We need to go back to the land!" cried the surviving animals.

"And we need to go back to the sea!" cried the surviving fish.

They never switched places again.

41. THE CRABS AND THE FOX

The crabs found a fox weeping on the beach.

"What's wrong?" they asked.

"The other foxes were planning to devour you," he replied, "but I said we should not harm such pretty creatures."

The crabs were glad to meet a friendly fox.

Then the fox said to the crabs, "Let's go dancing in the moonlight!"

The fox danced happily together with the crabs.

"Come dance, my friends, come, come!"

The fox and the crabs danced up the sand and into the grass-covered dunes… where all the other foxes were waiting.

And so the foxes devoured the crabs, every last one.

42. THE CRANE AND THE FISH

The lake was drying up.

"Don't worry, fish-friends!" said a crane. "I'll carry you to my home, a big lake nearby."

"Thank you!' said the fish, and she carried them off one by one.

But the crane wasn't relocating the fish; she was devouring them.

Finally only a crab remained.

"Come on!" said the crane.

Then, as they were landing, the crab looked down and saw fishbones, so he grabbed the crane's neck with his pincers.

"Let go!" the crane said, but the crab squeezed.

SNAP!

The crane died, and the crab lived happily ever after in the big lake.

43. BIG-WIT, HALF-WIT, AND WITLESS

There were three fish living in a pond: Big-Wit, Half-Wit, and Witless.

Fishermen came to their pond, looking for fish to catch.

Big-Wit realized the danger at once and went swimming through the pond's outlet before the fishermen blocked it up. Thus he made his escape.

Half-Wit was unsure what to do, but finally he pretended to be dead, floating on top of the water, and the fishermen had no interest in a rotten fish carcass.

As for Witless, terror made him splash in the water, so the fishermen seized him and he became fish stew for the fishermen's dinner.

44. THE TWO FISH AND THE FROG

Two fish named Smart and Very-Smart lived in a remote lake together with a frog named Not-So-Smart.

One day fishermen discovered the lake. "We'll come fish here tomorrow," the fishermen said.

The frog was very upset. "What can we do?" he said.

"Don't worry!" said the fish named Very-Smart. "We'll figure it out tomorrow." The fish named Smart nodded confidently. "We're smart!"

But Not-So-Smart decided to leave the lake right away and hide nearby.

The next morning he saw the fishermen hauling Very-Smart and Smart away in their nets.

"Sometimes it's better not to be so smart!" said the frog.

45. THE FROG IN THE WELL

A frog was born in a well and lived there all her life.

Another frog was born and lived in a lake.

The lake-frog went exploring, and when she hopped up on the edge of the well, she fell in.

She tried to tell the well-frog what the lake was like. "It's big!" she said.

"As big as this?" asked the well-frog, hopping from one side of the well to the other.

"Bigger!" said the lake-frog.

"But there's nothing bigger than the well. You've lost your mind!" shouted the well-frog. "That 'lake' is something you dreamed; it can't be real."

46. THE FROG-KING IN THE WELL

The frog-king ruled the frogs of the well. The king had many enemies, so he hopped out of the well and found a snake.

"Snake," he said, "please kill my enemies."

"But I cannot swim!" replied the snake.

"You can hide in a hole in the wall of the well," explained the frog-king. "I'll show you my enemies, but you must spare my friends and family."

So the greedy snake ate all the frog-king's enemies.

Then his friends.

Then his family.

Terrified, the frog-king ran away.

"Frog-King, come back!" shouted the snake.

But the frog-king now knew not to listen.

47. THE SNAKE AND THE FROG

A snake and a frog lived in the same pond, and they became friends.

"I'll teach you how to hiss!" the snake said to the frog one day.

"And I'll teach you how to croak!" said the frog to the snake.

After the snake learned how to croak, he would hide in the reeds and croak just like a frog, luring the other frogs to come near, and then he would eat them.

Eventually, the other frogs learned about the snake's trick, so the snake had no more frogs to eat.

That's when he decided to eat his so-called friend.

48. THE FROG-KING RIDES THE SNAKE

A snake came to the frogs and said, "A brahmin has cursed me to be your vehicle. I must carry you on my back wherever you want to go."

The king of the frogs jumped on the snake's back. The other frogs did the same, and the snake did indeed carry them wherever they told him to go.

The next day, however, the snake was moving slowly.

"I'm hungry!" the snake said.

"Eat some frogs!" suggested the frog king.

Day by day the snake ate the frogs until only the king was left.

And then the snake ate him too.

49. THE SNAKE AND THE ANTS

There was a mighty snake, the terror of the neighborhood. Nobody dared to challenge this snake.

Then one day the snake decided to slither through a narrow space between some rocks, and there he got stuck, bleeding where the rocks had scraped his skin.

Drawn by the smell of blood, the ants began to swarm. The ants were tiny, but they came in hundreds. Then in thousands.

The snake squirmed and thrashed as the ants crawled all over him, but there was nothing he could do.

And thus the tiny ants killed the mighty snake, bite by bite by bite.

50. DEER, TIGER, AND CROCODILE

A deer had gone to drink, and a tiger lay in wait in the bushes nearby.

"That deer will make a delicious meal," the tiger thought.

Meanwhile, there was a crocodile in the water who also had his eyes on the deer.

As the deer finished drinking, the tiger leaped, but he missed and fell.

Then, as he tumbled with a splash into the water, the crocodile seized him.

They fought, and both died of their wounds.

The deer, watching the unexpected drama, exclaimed, "It's a good day for the deer when the tiger and the crocodile destroy one another."

51. THE RABBIT AND THE COCONUT

Rabbit slept under a coconut-tree, and a coconut fell on his head.

"The sky's falling!" Rabbit shouted. He jumped and ran.

"What's wrong?" Deer asked.

"End of the world! The sky's falling!" shrieked Rabbit, and Deer ran with him.

They met Fox. "What's wrong?" she asked.

Rabbit panted, "Sky falling! End of world!"

Now Rabbit, Deer, and Fox were running.

Monkey, Leopard, Elephant… all running!

Lion stopped them. "Who says it's the end of the world?"

They pointed at Rabbit, and Rabbit took Lion to the tree.

"A coconut fell down!" Lion roared. "It's not the end of the world."

52. THE FOX IN THE FLOOD

A fox had fallen into a rushing river.

"Help!" the fox shrieked. "It's the end of the world! A flood! Save yourselves! The end of the world!"

A man standing on the riverbank heard the fox's cries of alarm. He grabbed a branch and extended it to the fox, and then he pulled the fox to shore.

"Thank you, good sir!" said the fox.

"But what about the end of the world?" said the man. "Your words scared me!"

"Well, the world was ending," said the fox. "My world anyway!"

And with that, the fox scampered off into the woods.

53. THE HORSE TIED TO A TREE

A traveler tied his horse to a tree and lay down to sleep.

A thief stole the horse and returned to rob the traveler too, but the traveler woke up unexpectedly.

"Where's my horse?" he shouted.

"The tree ate him," said the thief.

"Impossible!" retorted the traveler. "See that fox? She'll tell us what happened."

"I didn't see the tree eat the horse," said the fox, "because I was too busy watching flames shoot forth from the pond over there."

"But flames can't shoot forth from ponds," said the thief.

"No more than trees can eat horses," said the fox.

54. THE TIGER AND THE FOX

A tiger found a fox in a trap.

"What are you doing there?" he asked.

"I did this for you!" replied the fox. "I'm luring men here so you can eat them."

"How kind of you!" said the tiger, who went to wait in the bushes.

The hunters came and found the fox.

"I've lured the tiger here so you can kill him," said the fox. "He's there in the bushes."

"How kind of you!' said the hunters, who then let the fox go.

"Good luck, hunters!" shouted the fox as she ran off. "And good luck to you, tiger!"

55. THE TIGER AND THE GOLDEN BANGLE

An old tiger lived beside a pond.

When a traveler passed nearby, the tiger shouted, "Here! Take this golden bangle!"

The traveler was surprised by the tiger's words. "Show me the bangle!" he said.

The tiger showed him.

"But can I trust you?" asked the traveler.

"I'm old," said the tiger, "with no teeth and no claws. Before I die, I'm giving away my wealth. Come! Cross the pond and take the bangle."

When the man waded into the pond, he got stuck in the mud.

"I'll help you!" said the tiger.

So saying, the tiger pounced and devoured him.

56. THE TWIN PARROTS

A parrot gave birth to twins with identical green bodies, blue heads, red wings, and yellow tails. Bandits carried away one chick; a monk took the other.

A king rode through the forest one day. He passed the bandits' camp, and a parrot squawked, "Bind him! Kill him!" The king saw the parrot was green, blue, red, and yellow.

He then passed a hermitage. "Honor the king!" a parrot squawked.

"I saw a parrot just like you: green, blue, red, and yellow," said the king. "But he spoke differently."

"We were born as twins," replied the parrot, "but raised differently."

57. THE CAPTIVE FAWN

A prince went hunting and caught a fawn which he took home as a pet.

The fawn, however, was unhappy: he longed to return to the herd.

One day the fawn shouted, "Woe is me! What is this nightmare? Where's my herd?"

This terrified the prince. "A speaking fawn is an evil portent," he thought, so he summoned his magicians and wise men.

"Save me from this demon!" he pleaded.

"Just listen to the words," said one of the wise men, "and let the fawn go."

So the prince freed the fawn, and he was not troubled by portents again.

58. THE KING AND HIS MONKEY

A king appointed a pet monkey to be his royal sword-bearer and bodyguard.

One day, the king went into the royal gardens. The day was hot, so the king decided to nap in the shade of a tree.

"Let no one disturb me!" he commanded the monkey.

After a while, a bumblebee flew by and landed on the king's nose. The monkey raised his sword and brought it down upon the offending insect, lest it disturb the king.

He killed the bee, but he also killed the king.

Thus a foolish friend is more dangerous than the most dangerous enemy.

59. THE MONKEYS AND THE GARDENER

The royal gardener wanted a vacation.

There were some monkeys living in the garden, so the gardener decided to put the monkeys in charge while he was gone.

"Make sure you water all the plants!" he told the monkeys.

"We should inspect the roots first," commanded the chief of the monkeys. "The deep roots need lots of water; the shallow roots not so much."

So the monkeys inspected the roots carefully, pulling them up out of the ground to look at them.

The gardener came back from vacation to find all the plants were dead, uprooted by the foolish monkeys.

60. MONKEY SEE, MONKEY DO

One day a monkey in a tree watched while the woodcutters worked.

When the woodcutters went to eat their lunch, he jumped down on the log where they were using wedges to split the wood.

"Why did they put this thing here?" he wondered. Monkeys are curious creatures, and this monkey was more curious than most.

So, the monkey grabbed the wedge and pulled it out… and then the log snapped shut on his privates! He was trapped, and it was all because of his own foolishness.

Learn from the monkey: do not meddle in things you know nothing about.

61. THE MONKEY AND THE SPARROW

There was a sparrow who lived in a nest high up in a tree.

One day, she saw a monkey shivering at the foot of the tree.

"If you are cold," she said, "you should build a house!"

The monkey did not listen to her, but the sparrow kept giving him advice.

"I can tell you how to build a house!" she chirped.

"I have a very nice house!" she chirped more loudly.

"A house will keep you warm!" she kept on chirping.

Finally, the monkey got so angry that he climbed up the tree and destroyed the sparrow's house.

62. THE WILD GEESE

Some wild geese lived in a tree.

The oldest goose noticed a vine growing up the tree. "We must tear down that vine before a human climbs it!" she said, but the young geese mocked her.

A hunter later climbed the tree and placed a snare there which trapped all the geese.

"Play dead!" said the old goose.

This time, the other geese did as she said.

The hunter found the birds all dead – or so he thought – and tossed them to the ground.

Then, as he was climbing down the tree, they all flew away to safety!

63. THE KING OF THE DOVES

A hunter spread a net on the ground, covering it with grain.

When doves rushed to eat the grain, their feet were caught. The more they thrashed, the more tightly they were trapped.

"Be calm!" said the dove-king. "Use your wings instead."

Together, the doves flapped their wings and rose up, carrying the net, while the hunter shouted at them angrily.

The doves then flew to the home of their friend: a mouse.

"Help us, mouse!" said the dove-king, and the mouse chewed through the knots and freed all the doves from the net.

The moral: Cooperate, and be kind.

64. THE GADFLY AND THE LION

A gadfly found a lion sleeping in his den. She bit the lion's lip and drank his blood.

The lion awoke and grabbed the gadfly.

"Mercy!" begged the gadfly. "Let me go and I'll do you a favor someday."

The lion scoffed at the idea of a gadfly doing him a favor, but he let the creature go.

Some days later, the gadfly saw hunters creeping towards the lion's den. She once again bit the lion, waking him. "You must go," shouted the gadfly, "or else the hunters will trap you here!"

The lion thus escaped, thanks to a gadfly.

65. TURTLE, DEER, MOUSE, AND CROW

A turtle, deer, mouse, and crow were all friends.

One day a hunter caught the turtle and carried her away in a sack.

The mouse advised the deer to lie down in the hunter's path, pretending to be dead, while the crow pretended to peck at her dead body.

When the hunter saw the deer, he put down the sack, got out his knife and advanced towards the deer.

The mouse quickly gnawed a hole in the sack so the turtle escaped, while the crow flapped in the hunter's face till the deer got away.

The moral: Friendship is powerful.

66. DEER, CROW, AND JACKAL

A deer and a crow lived as friends.

The deer then befriended a jackal. The crow, however, mistrusted the jackal.

The next day the jackal led the deer into a snare.

"Help!" yelled the deer.

The crow flew up and squawked so loudly that a hunter came running. "Pretend you're dead!" the crow whispered to the deer.

The deer lay down as if dead, and when the hunter freed her from the snare, she leaped up and ran off.

The hunter shot at the deer, but hit the jackal instead, killing him.

The deer no longer made friends with jackals.

67. THE HUNTER AND THE JACKAL

A hunter shot a deer and was carrying it home when he saw a boar. "I'll catch the boar too!"

The hunter shot the boar, but only wounded it.

The boar attacked, killing the hunter, and then died of its wounds.

When the boar fell, it happened to crush a snake to death.

A jackal strolled by.

"What a feast!" he exclaimed. "Human, deer, boar and snake! I don't want to miss out on anything edible. I can even eat the bowstring!"

But when the greedy jackal gnawed the bowstring, the bow snapped, struck the jackal and killed him too.

68. THE GOOSE AND THE CROW

A goose and a crow lived together in a tree.

One hot day, a hunter decided to rest beneath that tree.

As he slept, the sun moved, exposing his face, so the kindly goose shaded the man's face from the sun with her wings.

Meanwhile, the wicked crow pooped down on the man's face and then flew away, cackling with delight.

When the man awoke, he wiped away the poop and, looking up, he saw the goose.

"You cursed bird!" he shouted.

He then grabbed his gun and shot the goose dead.

The moral: Be careful what company you keep.

69. THE MONKEY AND THE GOAT

A wily monkey once stole a workman's rice and lentils.

After gobbling almost all the food, the monkey then set about laying the blame on someone else.

"The goat would make a likely culprit," the monkey thought to himself.

So the monkey fed the rest of the rice and lentils to the goat, making sure to smear food all over the goat's mouth and in his beard.

"Thank you, monkey!" said the gullible goat.

When the workman returned, he blamed the goat.

"You cursed beast!" he shouted as he beat the poor goat, while the monkey just laughed and laughed.

70. THE LOUSE AND THE FLEA

There was once a louse who lived in the king's palace.

She grew fat sucking on the king's blood, but because she nibbled gently, the king never realized she was there.

It was a good life.

One day, a flea dropped in. "What a nice bed this is!" he said.

The louse protested. "The king will feel your unfamiliar bite. Go away!"

But the flea didn't go away, and he bit the king while he slept.

The king was furious, and he called his servants to come inspect the bed. The flea escaped, but the louse was caught and killed.

71. THE TURTLE AND THE PEACOCK

A turtle saw a peacock dancing beside a pond.

"I want to dance with you," said the turtle.

The peacock looked at him doubtfully. "You're too slow, and you have no feathers to compare with mine."

"I'll surprise you," said the turtle, "for my shell is truly colorful and, though slow, I am graceful."

So the turtle danced with the peacock, and the peacock had to admire his lovely shell and steady pace.

A hunter, however, discovered them there.

The peacock flew to safety in a tree, but the hunter caught and killed the turtle before he reached the pond.

72. THE TURTLE IN THE LAKE

The princes shouted, "Father, we saw a terrible lake-monster!"

The king's guards went and caught the monster.

It was only a turtle, but the princes had never seen a turtle before and it frightened them.

"How shall we kill it?" the king asked.

"Crush it!" said the first prince.

"Burn it!" said the second.

"Drown it!" said the third.

Then the turtle shrieked, "Don't drown me! Crush me, burn me, but please don't drown me!"

"Drown the turtle!" the king commanded.

The guards threw the turtle into the lake.

The turtle shouted "Home at last!" as he happily swam away.

73. THE TURTLE AND THE TWO BIRDS

A turtle once befriended two birds, and the three friends lived together at a lake.

The lake was drying up, so the birds offered to carry the turtle away.

"You bite the middle of this stick, and we'll carry the ends in our beaks," they said. "But you must keep your mouth closed. Don't open your mouth, okay?"

"Okay!" the turtle said.

They soared into the sky: the plan worked!

But then people on the ground started laughing.

"That turtle looks ridiculous up there!" they said.

The turtle opened his mouth to rebuke them and thus plunged to his death.

74. THE DONKEY AND THE JACKAL

A farmer allowed his donkey to wander freely at night.

One night the donkey met a jackal and they became friends.

Together, they broke into a cucumber field and ate all the cucumbers they wanted.

Then the donkey decided to sing.

"Don't do that!" hissed the jackal.

But the donkey insisted on singing. "I have a lovely singing voice," he said. "You're just jealous!"

The jackal hid in the bushes and watched. The donkey sang very loudly, and finally the villagers came and cudgeled him to death.

"Music is all well and good," thought the jackal, "but silence is safer."

75. THE DONKEY AND THE TIGER-SKIN

There was a laundryman who had a donkey.

One day, the laundryman found a tiger-skin in the jungle and put the tiger-skin on his donkey.

"The farmers will be afraid of my tiger," he thought.

Wearing the tiger-skin, the donkey was able to graze in the barley-fields at night, getting fat on the farmers' barley.

But one night, the donkey heard the bray of a she-donkey, and he could not resist: he also started to bray!

The farmers realized this was not a tiger, but a donkey, so they beat the poor donkey and drove him away from their fields.

76. THE DONKEY AND THE WATCHDOG

A thief came to rob a house.

The donkey said to the watchdog, "You should bark!"

"Our master treats us badly," said the dog. "Why should I bark?"

Since the dog wouldn't bark, the donkey brayed.

This scared the thief, but the master didn't know anything about that. Instead, he was furious that the donkey woke him up. In his rage, he beat the donkey so badly that the donkey died.

The dog shook his head sadly. "The donkey should have listened to me and kept his mouth shut."

The thief returned the next night.

The dog did not bark.

77. THE BRAVE MONGOOSE

A brahmin and his wife had a pet mongoose.

One day the woman went out.

"Watch the baby!" she told her husband.

Then the man went out.

"Watch the baby!' he told the mongoose.

Then... a snake came!

The brave mongoose killed the snake, overturning the baby's cradle in their struggle.

When the woman returned, she saw the overturned cradle and the mongoose covered in blood. Thinking it had killed her baby, she killed the mongoose.

Then she heard her baby crying and found the remains of the snake, and so she wept for the terrible mistake she had made.

78. THE PILGRIMS AND THE JEWELS

Three pilgrims found some jewels in the road.

"Let's eat them for safekeeping!" they said.

A beggar lurking nearby heard this. He joined their party, planning to cut them open that night.

But then a robber ambushed them.

"Jewels! Jewels!" squawked the robber's parrot.

The robber seized and stripped them. No jewels.

The parrot kept squawking, "Jewels!"

"I'll cut you open!" shouted the robber.

The beggar, racked by guilt for his wicked plan, shouted, "The parrot lies! Cut me first; you'll see!"

The robber cut him open.

No jewels.

So the robber let the pilgrims go ... and punished the parrot.

79. THE BANDIT'S GHOST

A bandit stole the village bell and fled to the hills where a tiger killed him. Whenever people heard the bell ringing, they whispered in fear, "It's the bandit's ghost!"

But it was only a monkey ringing the bell.

The village-chief offered a reward for anyone brave enough to defeat the ghost and retrieve the bell.

A wise woman guessed the truth.

"I can defeat the ghost!" she proclaimed.

She took no weapons, just fruit. She fed the fruit to the monkey, and thus she snatched the bell.

She returned to the village ringing the bell and claimed her reward.

80. THE RATS IN THE HOUSE

A foolish man saw there were rats in his house.

He was determined to destroy the rats, so he set his own house on fire.

His house burned down to the ground.

But the rats escaped by running to the house next door, so the man burned down that house too.

"You won't escape me, you rats!" he shouted.

But the rats just ran into the next house, so the man set that house on fire as well.

And the next. And the next.

Give him enough time and that fool will burn down all the houses in the world.

81. THE RATS AND THE JACKAL

The Buddha was born as a rat, and there was a jackal who liked to eat rats.

To trick them, the jackal pretended to be a sadhu, gazing at the sun, standing on one leg, eating no food.

Each day the rats would run by the saintly jackal, and each day the jackal grabbed the last rat running by.

The Buddha suspected something was wrong, so he brought up the rear.

When the jackal tried to grab him, the Buddha shouted, "You evil hypocrite!" He jumped at the jackal's throat and killed him, and the rats enjoyed a great feast.

82. THE JACKAL IN THE ELEPHANT

In another lifetime, the Buddha was again born as a jackal.

One day, this jackal found an elephant carcass.

"Food!" he shouted happily.

He gnawed the elephant's trunk; not much meat there.

The tusk was like bone.

The ear was tough.

The feet were hard as rocks.

Then the jackal crawled inside where the meat was soft to eat. He stayed in there for days.

Meanwhile, the summer heat made the carcass shrink.

The jackal couldn't get out. He was trapped!

Finally it rained.

As the carcass expanded again, he escaped.

"I'll never be so greedy again!" the Buddha vowed.

83. THE JACKAL AND THE CORPSE

The Buddha was again born as a jackal, and he made his home in the cremation fields amidst the corpses.

A wicked man who wanted to kill the jackal had gone there and lay on the ground, club in hand, pretending to be dead.

The jackal approached, but he suspected this man was not really dead.

He grabbed the club in his teeth and tugged. The man tightened his grip, and the jackal let go.

"Human, if you were dead, you wouldn't have tightened your grip."

The man then sprang up, but he was too late: the Buddha had escaped.

84. THE JACKAL AND THE LION

The Buddha was once born as a lion.

A jackal asked to be this lion's servant. The lion agreed, and the jackal grew fat eating food the lion killed.

As time went by, the jackal thought he was as strong and mighty as a lion. "I'm ready to kill an elephant on my own!" he boasted.

The lion warned him of the danger, but the jackal wouldn't listen.

Then, when the jackal tried to bite an elephant's foot, the elephant crushed the jackal to death.

"Foolish jackal," said the Buddha, "you learned your limitations at the cost of your life."

85. THE DEER AND HIS NEPHEW

The Buddha was born as a deer.

The deer's sister said to her son, "Go to your uncle and learn the tricks you need to stay safe from hunters."

But the young deer didn't listen to his mother.

The Buddha said to him, "Nephew, there are things you must learn to stay safe. I will teach you."

But the young deer didn't listen to his uncle.

He then fell into a hunter's trap and was killed.

"Brother," said the Buddha's sister, weeping, "why didn't you teach him?"

"I couldn't teach him," said the Buddha, "because he didn't want to learn."

86. THE TWO OXEN

The Buddha was born as an ox. His name was Big Red, and he had a brother named Little Red.

They lived on a farm together with other animals, including a pig.

The oxen worked hard, but the pig didn't work; the pig just ate.

And ate.

And ate.

Little Red was jealous, but Big Red told him, "That pig is eating the food of death; they are fattening him up for a wedding."

Big Red was right: when the wedding day came, that was the end of the pig, and Little Red recognized the wisdom of the Buddha's words.

87. THE FISH AND THE CRANE

The Buddha was once born as a fish, and through his good actions he became the king of the fish.

There was a crane who wanted to eat the fish, so he pretended to be asleep. The other fish were fooled, but the Buddha realized that the crane was their deadly enemy.

"My fellow fish," the Buddha said, "we must drive this wicked creature away, and it will take all of us working together. One, two, three… SPLASH."

At the Buddha's command, the fish all started splashing at the crane until he finally flew away to look for food elsewhere.

88. THE PARROT AND THE MANGOS

The Buddha was born as a parrot. He had a son. When he grew up, the son cared for his elderly father, bringing him food.

One day the son flew to an island full of mango trees. He brought back a mango.

"Beware, my son," said the parrot's father. "That is too far; do not go to the mango island."

But the son did not listen. He flew again to the mango island, and then he grew so tired flying home that he fell into the ocean, and a fish ate him.

The Buddha waited, but his son never returned.

89. THE WOODPECKER AND THE LION

The Buddha was once born as a woodpecker.

One day this woodpecker saw a lion, groaning in pain.

"Help me, woodpecker!" shouted the lion. "Extract the bone stuck in my throat, and I'll give you a reward!"

The woodpecker agreed, but he was cautious.

First, he propped the lion's mouth open with a stick, and only then did he extract the bone.

After emerging from the lion's mouth, he knocked away the stick.

"What's my reward?" the woodpecker asked.

"Escaping my teeth is reward enough!" the lion snarled.

Thus the Buddha knew he was wise not to trust the lion.

90. THE QUAIL CHICK

The Buddha was born as a tiny quail chick.

The chick lived in a nest, fed by his mother and father, and he could not fly yet.

Then one day, a huge fire swept through the forest, and the mother and father quail flew away in fear.

Because the quail chick could not fly, he summoned the power of his past Buddha lives and spoke forth. "In the name of Truth," shouted the little bird, "I defy you, Fire! Turn back now!"

And so the flames of the forest fire were extinguished by the miraculous power of the Buddha's words.

91. THE QUAIL AND THE HUNTER

The Buddha was born as a quail.

A hunter caught the Buddha and his flock, and he put them in cages, feeding them well and fattening them to sell.

"If we don't eat, we'll grow thin," the Buddha thought, "and that might save us."

So he told the others, "Don't eat!"

But they ate the food and grew fat, and then the hunter sold them.

Meanwhile, the Buddha grew thin and lay motionless in the cage.

"Is it dead?" the hunter wondered.

He took the bird out to see what was wrong, and the Buddha jumped up and flew away.

92. THE BIRDS BY THE LAKE

The Buddha was born as a bird, and he lived with other birds in a tree that stretched over a lake.

Some of the birds peed and pooped in the lake, and this made the great Naga-snake who lived in the lake angry.

The Naga made the waters of the lake boil, and he shot flames from his mouth into the branches of the tree.

"We must fly away!" said the Buddha, and the wise birds followed him to safety.

The foolish birds, however, stayed in the tree, peeing and pooping in the water, until they died in the flames.

93. THE BIRDS IN THE TREE

The Buddha was born as a bird and he lived together with a flock of birds in a mighty tree; the Buddha was the king of these birds.

The branches of the tree where the birds lived began to grind one against the other, producing sparks and smoke.

The king realized that this was the beginning of a fire, so he warned all the other birds. "We must fly away now!" he told them.

The wise birds listened, but the foolish birds ignored the Buddha's words.

The whole tree caught on fire, and the foolish birds perished in the flames.

94. THE CROW BY THE HIGHWAY

The Buddha was born as a bird and became their king.

There was a crow who hopped along the highway, eating the food that humans dropped there.

The bird-king warned all the birds that the human highway was dangerous, but the crow kept going there anyway, greedy for food.

One day as the crow was eating, she saw a caravan coming down the highway. "I'll fly away soon!" she said, but she kept on eating... and so she was crushed under the wheels of a wagon.

"The highway is dangerous," said the Buddha, "but being greedy is even more dangerous."

95. THE BIRD-KING AND THE PEACOCK

The Buddha was again born as a bird, and again he became their king.

The bird-king had a daughter, and the time had come for her to choose a husband.

She liked the beautiful peacock most of all.

"I want the peacock to be my husband," she said.

The peacock danced with excitement, and as he danced he exposed his private parts for all to see.

The birds were shocked!

The king of the birds said, "I can't let my daughter marry this bird. He is beautiful, but his dancing has led to disaster."

The peacock flew away in shame.

96. THE SWAN WITH THE GOLDEN FEATHERS

The Buddha was born as a man who had a wife and children.

When the man died, he was reborn as a swan with golden feathers.

The swan flew home and gave his wife a feather. "I'll return soon and give you more," he promised.

But when he returned, his wife plucked all his feathers.

"Wicked woman, what have you done?" he cried, and the feathers in her hands became ordinary white swan feathers.

The wife threw the plucked swan into the garbage.

Then, when the Buddha's feathers grew back – white now, not golden – he flew away and never returned.

97. THE DRUMMER AND THE BANDITS

The Buddha was born as a drummer, and his son was a drummer too.

Returning from a festival, they had to cross a forest full of bandits.

"I'll scare the bandits by beating the drum constantly," said the boy.

"No!" said the Buddha. "Just beat the drum slowly now and then, like the drummer for a great lord."

At the first drumbeats, the bandits fled, but when the son kept on drumming, they became curious. Then, when they saw a father and son traveling alone, they attacked and robbed them.

Too much, even of a good thing, is not good.

98. THE MONK AND HIS SNAKE

There was once a Buddhist monk who had adopted a poisonous snake, keeping the snake in a cage like a pet.

The Buddha warned this monk that the snake couldn't be trusted, but the monk did not listen.

"I can't live without my snake friend," he said.

One day the monk went to feed his snake. "Come here, my dear snake," he said as he opened the cage. "I have food for you!"

Hunger had made the snake impatient, and it bit the monk on the hand.

Thus the foolish monk died, and the snake slithered away into the forest.

99. THE BUDDHA AND THE MANTRA

The Buddha had taught one of his young disciples a mantra for bringing the dead to life.

"Use it carefully," the Buddha warned him.

Later on, the young man, together with some other disciples, went into the jungle. There they found a dead tiger.

"I will bring this dead tiger to life!" the disciple shouted, and then he spoke the mantra.

A living tiger sprang up, killed the young disciple, and ran off.

The other disciples returned to the Buddha and told him what had happened.

"Before people do favors for villains," the Buddha said, "they should consider the outcome."

100. THE THREE FRIENDS AND THE TIGER

There were three friends making their way through a jungle when they were attacked by a tiger.

The first friend shouted, "We are lost!"

The second friend shouted, "God, please save us!"

The third friend shouted, "We need to climb a tree!"

Here is what you need to understand about these three men.

The first man did not know God at all.

The second man was a seeker of God.

The third man had an ecstatic and complete love of God. His goal was not to save himself from the tiger, but to spare his beloved any trouble or worry.

101. THE ELEPHANT-DRIVER

A guru and his disciples lived in the forest.

One day, a mad elephant came rampaging through the trees.

"Get out of the way!" yelled the elephant-driver.

All the disciples fled to safety, but one disciple didn't move.

The elephant grabbed him and hurled him against a tree; the disciple barely survived.

"Why didn't you run?" the guru asked his disciple later.

"You taught us that all things are God," he said. "Why run from God?"

"Yes, the elephant is God, but the elephant-driver is God also!" explained the guru. "You should have listened to God in his elephant-driver form."

102. THE PILGRIM AND THE SNAKE

A pilgrim converted a cobra to the holy life.

"Do no harm," he told the cobra, "and don't bite!"

The snake nodded, and the pilgrim departed.

The village boys, however, grew bold and pelted the snake with rocks.

Its bones broken, the snake could barely slither in and out of its hole.

When the pilgrim returned, he was shocked by the snake's condition.

"The boys attack me," it said. "But I keep my vow!"

"I told you no biting, but I didn't forbid hissing!" the pilgrim exclaimed. "Do no harm, but you must hiss if someone threatens to harm you."

103. THE TWO MEN AND THE MANGOS

Two men went into a mango orchard.

One man immediately began to count the number of trees and the number of mangos on the trees, and even the number of leaves, estimating how much might be harvested, what the mangos would weigh, and so on.

The other man went to the orchard's owner and befriended him. Then, at the invitation of his host, he began to eat the mangos. They were delicious!

Be like that man: befriend the Creator and enjoy the gifts of creation. What is the good of numbers and calculations when you could be eating mangos instead?

104. THE TWO FRIENDS IN TOWN

Two friends went to town together.

"Let's go listen to a reading of Holy Scripture!" said one.

"I think I'll go to a whorehouse!" said the other.

The man who went to the reading was bored; he wished he had gone to the whorehouse.

The man who went to the whorehouse felt ashamed; he wished he had gone to the reading.

The Angel of Death came for them both at that moment, taking the man in the whorehouse to heaven, and taking the other man down to hell.

God looks at your deeds, and he also looks at your heart.

105. THE PRICELESS DIAMOND

A wealthy man possessed a priceless diamond.

"Take this to the market," he said to his servant, "and see what people are willing to pay for it."

The eggplant-vendor offered twenty pounds of eggplants.

"Not more?" asked the servant.

"That is a lot for this small bauble!" the vendor replied.

The clothes-dealer offered a thousand rupees.

"Not more?" asked the servant.

"That is too much already!" he said.

And so on, until the servant finally approached a jeweler who said, "I'll give you everything I have!"

So it is with God: each comprehends within the limits of their own experience.

106. THE FISH AND THE FLOWERS

A fishmonger ran into her cousin, a flower-seller, in the marketplace.

"You've sold all your fish, and I've sold all my flowers," said the flower-seller. "Come have dinner with me! You can stay the night."

The fishmonger gladly accepted.

She left her fishbasket at the door of her cousin's house.

They ate dinner, and then they went to bed.

During the night, the fishmonger tossed and turned. The smell of flowers was suffocating!

She finally went and got her fishbasket, putting it in the bed beside her. Smelling the familiar smell of fish, she was able to sleep at last.

107. THE PILGRIM COUPLE

A husband and wife decided they would renounce the world and spend their remaining years on a holy pilgrimage.

One day the husband, walking ahead of his wife, saw a diamond lying in the dust of the road. He scratched at the ground, trying to bury the diamond so his wife wouldn't see it and lapse back into worldly desires.

His wife then noticed what he was doing and rebuked him. "Why did you do that? Do you still see a difference between diamonds and the dust of the road? You must look beyond," she said. "There is no difference."

108. THE HOLY MAN AND THE DOG

There was a holy man who lived on food given to him in charity.

One day when he received some food, he sat down next to a dog, and they ate together. The man took a morsel of food and placed it in the dog's mouth, then he put a morsel in his own mouth, back and forth, taking turns.

The villagers saw this and started laughing, thinking he was a lunatic.

The holy man also laughed and he said, "God sits with God; God feeds God! You, God, are laughing, and I, God, am laughing! Whatever is… is God."

109. THE LIZARD ON THE TREE

There was a tree in the center of a village.

One man told another about the green lizard he saw on the tree.

"It's not green!" said another man. "I saw that lizard, and it's red."

Another man chimed in. "No, the lizard is brown."

Or black or orange or yellow.

The people were all arguing about the color of the lizard.

Finally, they went to the tree and found a man sitting there, a stranger to the village. He explained to them about the chameleon's many colors, and then he added, "In the same way, people argue about God."

110. THE WOODCUTTER'S DREAM

A woodcutter was napping when his friend shook him and said, "Hey, wake up!"

"Why did you wake me up?" complained the woodcutter. "I dreamed I was a king, the ruler of a great kingdom and father to many children. I sat happily on my throne and administered justice to all my subjects. Why did you destroy my happy state?"

"But it was just a dream!" protested his friend. "What does it matter?"

"You fool!" said the woodcutter. "You understand nothing. Being a king is just as real, and not real, as my being a woodcutter."

So teaches the Vedanta.

111. THE FARMER'S DREAM

A farmer and his wife doted on their young son, but one day he fell ill and died.

The mother was stricken with grief; the farmer, however, did not cry.

When she asked him why he was not grieving for their son, he said, "Last night, I dreamed I was a king, and I had eight fine sons. Then, in the morning, I woke up. Who should I weep for? The eight sons in the dream who vanished? Our son who died? It is all Maya; it is all illusion."

The farmer then took his plow and went to work.

112. THE HILL OF SUGAR

You cannot know all of God.

You are an ant who found a hill of sugar.

You rejoice! You eat a whole lump of sugar, and it fills your stomach completely. You barely manage to carry back a lump of sugar to your home, something to share with your fellow ants.

"Next time," you think to yourself, "I will bring back the whole sugar hill."

But you can't. You are just an ant.

Even the biggest ant, the most wise among the ant seekers, might be able to bring back two or three lumps of sugar, no more than that.

113. THE DOLL OF SALT

There was a doll made of salt who wanted to measure the ocean's depth.

"Take me to the ocean!" the doll said to its owner. "Put me in the ocean, and I will measure how deep it is. Then I will be able to tell others about the depth of the ocean."

The ocean was far off, many hundreds of miles away. But the owner did as the doll asked: she took the doll to the ocean.

Then, when she put the doll into the ocean's water, the doll began to dissolve.

The doll disappeared.

The doll was the ocean.

114. THE SEEKER AND HIS FAMILY

A man desired to follow his guru, but love of family held him back.

"Go home and take this pill," said the guru. "You will seem to be dead while hearing everything."

The man did so, and his family began to mourn.

The guru arrived and proclaimed, "I have medicine that will save him! He will drink it and live, but one of you will also have to drink, and you will die."

Mother, father, sisters, brothers... they all refused. "What's done is done," they said.

Having heard everything, the man awoke, and he left them to follow his guru.

115. THE THIEF-TURNED-SADHU

The king decided to choose a husband for his daughter from among the sadhus who meditated by the river.

A thief heard about this and disguised himself as a sadhu, hoping to marry the princess.

He sat among the sadhus when the king and princess came to inspect them. All the sadhus refused the king's offer.

As the thief sat there, watching one sadhu after another reject wealth and power, preferring the spiritual life, he was moved to become a sadhu himself.

"Will you marry the princess?" asked the king.

"No," said the thief-turned-sadhu, and with the sadhus he remained.

116. THE FISHERMAN-TURNED-SADHU

A fisherman was poaching fish from a rich man's lake at night.

The watchmen discovered him. "Stop!" they yelled.

The fisherman ran, and then to hide himself he covered his body with ashes and sat beneath a tree as if he were a sadhu.

By morning word had already spread that a sadhu had arrived. People came to see the sadhu under the tree, bringing offerings of flowers and fruits, bowing reverently.

The fisherman-turned-sadhu felt at peace.

"I think I shall become a true sadhu after all," he thought to himself, "and I will be worthy of these people's devotion."

117. THE HOLY MAN BY THE ROADSIDE

A holy man lay by the side of the road in the dark of night, deep in meditation.

A passing thief saw him and said, "That thief exhausted himself in criminal activity and fell asleep here before he got home. I won't make his mistake!"

A passing drunkard saw him and said, "That drunkard collapsed in a stupor here in public. Shameful! I will make sure I get home before I pass out!"

Another holy man walked by and bowed down in reverence.

Only he could see what was in front of his eyes; the others could see only themselves.

118. THE TRAVELER AND THE TREE

A traveler lay down to rest by a tree, not suspecting it was Kalpavriksha, the wish-fulfilling tree.

Because the man was tired, he thought how nice it would be to have a bed. A bed appeared!

Then he thought how nice it would be to have food. Done!

A woman to rub his feet. Done!

"This is wonderful!" he thought. "How silly of me to have worried about this journey. I almost didn't come because the tigers scared me."

Just as soon as he thought of the tigers, a tiger appeared, and it attacked the traveler and killed him.

119. THE WISEST OF THE BRAHMINS

There were once four brahmins who went traveling. Along the road, they found the bones of a lion.

The first brahmin said a mantra to assemble the bones into a skeleton.

The second brahmin said a mantra to add flesh and skin to the skeleton.

"I will now give it life!" said the third brahmin.

"Wait a minute!" said the fourth brahmin, and he hurriedly climbed a tree.

The third brahmin then pronounced his mantra.

The lion woke up hungry and ate the three brahmins before running off into the jungle.

The fourth brahmin alone lived to tell the tale.

120. THE BRAHMIN AND HIS MOUSE-DAUGHTER

A brahmin rescued a mouse from a hawk and turned her into a girl.

She grew up and needed a husband.

"I want the most powerful husband!" she said.

The brahmin thought Sun was the most powerful.

"Sun, marry my daughter," he said.

"Cloud is more powerful," said Sun. "He covers me."

Cloud said, "Wind is more powerful; he pushes me."

Wind said, "Mountain is more powerful; he blocks me."

Mountain said, "The mouse is the most powerful; he gnaws my foundations."

"Make me a mouse again!" said the girl, and thus she married the most powerful husband: a mouse.

121. THE BRAHMIN AND HIS SNAKE-SON

A brahmin dreamed he would have a strong, handsome son, but his wife gave birth to a snake. They loved him nonetheless.

Time passed.

"He must marry!" said the mother, so the brahmin visited a distant relative.

"Marry your daughter to my strong and handsome son!" the brahmin proposed.

When the bride learned the groom was a snake, she said only, "Let fate bring what it may."

On their wedding night, the snake turned into a handsome man, shedding his skin as she watched. The bride's father threw the snakeskin in the fire, and the couple lived happily ever after.

122. THE SNAKE AND THE BRAHMIN'S WIFE

A wandering brahmin and his wife encountered a serpent.

The serpent ate the brahmin!

The wife wept. "How will I live now?"

The serpent spat out a golden cup. "Beg alms with this. If anyone refuses you, his head will explode."

"Then I beg you: return my husband, or your head will explode!"

The snake spit her husband out, and then turned into a gandharva, a heavenly being.

"I was cursed to be a serpent until a woman outwitted me," said the gandharva, and as he flew upwards, jewels rained down.

The brahmin and his wife were beggars no more.

123. THE FARMER AND THE SNAKE

A snake lived in a farmer's field, and the farmer made milk offerings to that snake.

The snake would drink the milk and leave a gold coin in exchange.

The farmer kept all this secret, but eventually he told his son. "You are old enough now; you go make the offering!"

When the boy saw the snake emerge from its hole with the gold coin, he concluded that the snake's den must be full of treasure. He struck the snake, intending to kill it, but instead the snake bit him.

The boy died, and the snake was never seen again.

124. THE MONK IN THE DREAM

A poor merchant saw a vision of a monk in a dream.

"I am money earned by your ancestors," said the monk. "You'll see me tomorrow. Kill me and take the money."

The next day, a monk came to the merchant as foretold. The merchant clubbed him to death, and the monk turned into a heap of gold coins.

The merchant's greedy neighbor happened to see this. He went to the nearby monastery and attacked the monks with a club.

Some died, some were wounded; none turned into gold coins.

The police arrested the neighbor for murder and hanged him.

125. THE THIEF AND THE DEMON

A thief was on his way to rob a brahmin's cow when he met a rakshasa-demon.

"You steal the cow, and I'll eat the brahmin!" said the demon.

When they arrived, the thief said, "I'll go get the cow."

"No," said the demon, "the noise will wake him. Me first!"

"No," said the thief. "Me first!"

They kept arguing.

"What's going on?" yelled the brahmin.

The thief said, "This demon wants to eat you!"

The demon said, "This thief wants to rob you!"

The brahmin pronounced a mantra to destroy the demon, and with a club he killed the thief.

126. THE BARBER AND THE FAIRY

A tree-fairy bestowed seven pots of gold on a barber.

When the barber got home, he discovered the seventh pot was only half-full. He felt compelled to fill the pot, so he put in all his own money. The pot was still just half-full.

He sold all his possessions, but even that did not fill the seventh pot.

He went begging, putting all the money in, but to no effect.

"This fairy's gift is a curse!" he shouted, and he told the fairy to take it all back.

So he lost all the gold, and all his own money too.

127. THE DIM-WITTED WEAVER

A weaver was chopping wood.

"I live here!" shouted a tree-fairy. "Stop, and I'll grant you a wish."

"I don't know what to wish for," the weaver said.

"I'll wait till you decide," replied the fairy.

The weaver's brother said, "Ask for a kingdom! You can be king!"

"No!" advised his wife. "Get two more arms and a second head so you can work two looms at once, weaving twice as much."

The weaver liked that idea, so he wished for extra arms and another head.

When the villagers saw him transformed, they screamed, "Monster!" and clubbed him to death.

128. SUNDA AND UPASUNDA

There were twin demon brothers, Sunda and Upasunda.

They tormented the whole world, but they honored Shiva devoutly, so Shiva had to grant them a boon.

"We want Parvati!" the demons shouted; Parvati was Shiva's wife.

So, Shiva gave them Parvati.

But then the demon brothers quarreled; each wanted Parvati for himself.

Shiva appeared to them disguised as a brahmin.

"Brahmin, judge between us!" they said.

"You must fight each other," he replied, "to see who is stronger."

Because the demons were equally strong, they killed each other in the fight.

Shiva and Parvati, along with the whole world, rejoiced.

129. RIDING SHIVA'S BULL

One night a man saw Shiva's bull descend from heaven. He grabbed the tail and rode up Mount Kailash where Shiva served him heavenly cakes cooked by Parvati herself.

He then rode the bull down and told his friend.

"Take me there!" his friend said.

So the next night he grabbed the tail, his friend grabbed onto his feet, and up they went.

The friend shouted, "How big were those cakes?"

"This big!" the man replied, letting go of the bull's tail to show him, and so the fools both fell down to earth.

They never saw Shiva's bull again.

130. THE TEETH OF SHIVA'S BULL

There was a mystical poet, deeply devoted to Shiva, who had composed a hymn in Shiva's name.

"What a marvelous hymn I have composed!" he thought to himself.

Then Shiva's faithful white bull Nandi appeared to the poet in a dream. The bull opened his mouth, revealing his teeth, and there, written on each tooth, were the words to the hymn.

The poet realized that he had composed nothing. The words were not his but had come to him from a past that has no beginning.

Thereafter when he sang the hymn, he thought only of Shiva, not of himself.

131. THE DOG IN SHIVA'S TEMPLE

There was a peasant woman who wanted to marry the king.

She followed the king when he left the palace and saw he bowed down to a sadhu.

"A sadhu will be an even better husband!"

She followed the sadhu to a temple where he kneeled before Shiva's image.

"I will marry Shiva instead!" she decided.

As she gazed at Shiva's image, a dog came and peed there.

"That dog is powerful!' she thought, so she followed the dog as it entered a peasant's house.

"He must be the most powerful of all!" she concluded, so she married the peasant.

132. SHIVA AND VISHNU

To defeat the demon Hiranyaksha, Lord Vishnu took the form of a mighty boar. In this form Vishnu defeated Hiranyaksha.

Next, Vishnu became a sow and gave birth to piglets, nursing them contentedly in his sow form.

The gods begged Vishnu to return to heaven. "Give up that body and come back to us!"

But Vishnu refused. "I'm staying here. I like this body."

Finally Lord Shiva came to free Vishnu from his incarnation. "Don't you remember who you are?" he said, and he struck Vishnu with his trident, destroying the sow's body.

Only then did Vishnu return to heaven.

133. MAYA: THE ILLUSION OF THE WORLD

Narada asked Lord Vishnu, "What is Maya?"

Vishnu ignored the question. "I'm thirsty," he said. "Bring me water."

Narada went to fetch water from a nearby river. There he saw a beautiful woman. He fell in love at first sight! They married and had children: two boys and a girl.

Years passed happily.

But then one day the river rose in a mighty flood.

Narada watched his beloved children drown, and then his wife.

As he sat on the riverbank weeping, Vishnu approached.

"Where is my water?" Vishnu asked. "And why are you weeping?"

At that moment, Narada understood Maya.

134. INDRA'S PARROT AND YAMA

Indra, King of the Gods, had a pet parrot.

"Yama, God of Death, is coming!" announced Indra's gatekeepers.

The parrot hid behind Indra, quaking with fear.

"What's wrong?" asked Indra.

"I fear Yama!" squawked the parrot.

Yama arrived.

"Greetings!" said Indra. "And please, I beg you: don't kill my parrot!"

"I decide nothing," said Yama. "That is for Kala, God of Time."

"Did you hear that, parrot?" said Indra. "Come out now; it's safe."

The parrot came out, and as soon as he beheld Yama, he died of fright.

"I did nothing!" Yama protested. "It must have been his time."

135. INDRA AND THE BRAHMIN

A brahmin saw a cow nibbling flowers in his garden.

Enraged, he beat the cow so severely that it died.

"It's not my fault, " the brahmin later claimed. "Lord Indra presides over the right hand; this is Indra's doing."

When Indra heard, he came to the garden in human disguise.

"What a lovely garden!" Indra said.

"I did all the work myself," boasted the brahmin.

As Indra praised the flowers, the fruits, and so on, the brahmin beamed.

Then Indra revealed himself. "If you take credit for all that, how can you blame me for the death of the cow?!"

136. GARUDA AND THE SNAKE-MAN

Fleeing the eagle-god Garuda, a snake disguised itself as a man and sought refuge with a prostitute.

"I charge one hundred elephants!" she said, just joking, but the snake-man conjured the elephants with magic.

The woman was amazed. "Who are you?" she asked.

The snake-man told her everything, but swore her to secrecy.

Garuda disguised himself as a man and also came to the prostitute's house.

"I already have a customer, and he paid a hundred elephants," she said, boasting. Then she added, "Don't tell anyone, but he's a snake!"

Garuda thus found the snake-man, killed him, and ate him.

137. THE SEAGULLS AND GARUDA

A seagull wanted to fly away to lay her eggs.

"No!" said her husband. "Lay them here in the sand."

"But the Ocean will take them."

"If he dares take them, I will drink him up!" replied the husband.

The Ocean took the eggs, so the seagull did as he promised. "I'll drink every last drop of you, Ocean!" he shouted.

"That's impossible with your small beak," said his wife. "We must ask Garuda to help us."

They prayed to Garuda, and the mighty eagle-god came down to the Ocean. "Give back the eggs!" Garuda commanded, and the Ocean obeyed.

138. AGNI AND VARUNA

The God of Fire, Agni, and the God of Rain, Varuna, were arguing about who was greater.

"Fire is greater than water!" said Agni.

"No!" said Varuna. "Water is greater than fire!"

They decided to have a contest to see who was right.

The God of Fire burned trees, crops and villages, but Varuna poured down rain and put out the fire. The God of Fire then fled into the mountain rocks, while rain kept pouring down.

Even now, Agni is hiding in the rocks; that's why when you strike rock with steel, sparks fly and you can make fire.

139. GANESHA IS BORN

The goddess Parvati created a son, Ganesha, to protect her while she bathed.

"Stand guard here," she told him. "Admit no one."

Her husband, Shiva, arrived, demanding to see his wife.

"No," said the boy, obeying his mother's orders. "She's bathing."

Enraged, Shiva cut off the boy's head.

"What have you done?" shrieked Parvati. "That was my son!"

Shiva sent his servants to bring back the head of the first creature they encountered, which was an elephant.

So they brought back the elephant's head, which Shiva placed on Ganesha's body.

That is why the god Ganesha has an elephant's head.

140. GANESHA AND THE CAT

One day little Ganesha found a cat in the woods.

He grabbed the cat's tail; then he let the cat go and chased her.

The poor cat fell into a mud puddle, and Ganesha laughed at the cat covered with mud.

He then went home to tell his mother Parvati what happened, but when he got there, he saw she too was covered with mud!

"Who did this?" asked Ganesha.

"You did," Parvati explained. "I am all life, and all life is me."

Ganesha bowed his head and promised her, "I will treat all life with respect from now on."

141. GANESHA AND KARTIKEYA

Kartikeya and Ganesha sat beside their mother, Parvati, who was wearing a necklace of beautiful jewels.

"My sons," she said, "I will give this necklace to the one who circles the Universe most quickly."

Kartikeya leaped on his peacock and flew off, certain he would win the race. "I'm so much faster than my fat brother with his elephant head!" he thought to himself.

Ganesha, meanwhile, walked in a circle around his mother and bowed down before her reverently, knowing she contained the whole Universe.

When Kartikeya returned, he saw Ganesha sitting beside Parvati, and he was wearing the necklace.

142. KUBERA AND GANESHA

Kubera invited Shiva to a feast.

"It will be the best feast ever!" he boasted.

To teach Kubera a lesson, Shiva sent his son Ganesha in his place.

Ganesha ate everything, and then asked, "Is there more?"

Kubera brought food from the kitchen.

Not enough.

From the pantry.

Not enough.

"Why isn't there more?"

Finally, Kubera went to Shiva and begged for help.

"Food served with love is truly filling," said Shiva.

So Kubera brought Ganesha a handful of rice. "I offer you this food with my whole heart," said Kubera.

Ganesha took the rice. "I am satisfied," he said.

143. DURGA PUJA

There was a wealthy man who arranged a feast to celebrate the Durga Puja each year, honoring the goddess. He sacrificed countless goats, and people came from all around to enjoy the goat curry and elaborate dishes that the man offered to his hungry guests, year after year after year.

Later on, though, the man stopped organizing the feasts, and his celebration of the Durga Puja was nothing like it had been in the past.

"Why do you no longer celebrate with a feast as before?" a friend asked him.

"Can't you see?" said the man. "My teeth are gone!"

144. THE STINGY MAN'S DINNER

A stingy man and his wife were about to eat dinner when a neighbor knocked.

"Say I'm dead!" the man hissed at his wife, and he stretched out in the bed.

"Alas, my dead husband!" she wailed.

The neighbor was suspicious, seeing dinner on the table. As a joke, he also wailed, calling the villagers to carry the man to the burning-grounds.

"Get up; they're going to cremate you," the wife hissed.

"No!" her husband hissed back.

So he lay there motionless while they carried him away and burned his body.

All because he didn't want to share his dinner.

145. THE POOR MAN'S POT OF HONEY

A poor man had gathered some honey. He suspended the honey-pot from a rafter and sat beneath it, daydreaming.

"When I sell this honey, I'll buy some chicks. They'll grow into chickens, lay eggs, more chicks, more chickens. With that money, I can buy land. Then I'll get a fine wife. We'll have a fine son. But if he ever disobeys me, that bad boy, I'll strike him with my cane..."

And as he lifted his cane to thrash the boy, he broke the honey-pot, spilling the honey all over himself.

Thus the man ended up more poor than before.

146. THE HERMIT IN THE FOREST

A hermit had retired to the forest, setting aside all the cares of the world, and a simple loincloth was his only possession.

But rats came and nibbled holes in the loincloth, so the hermit got a cat.

The cat needed milk, so the hermit acquired a cow.

To care for the cow, he employed a cowherd.

The cowherd wanted a house, so he built a house.

To clean the house, he needed a maid.

The maid was lonely living in the forest, so they built more houses.

The result was a village, and all the cares of the world.

147. THE GURU'S TWO DISCIPLES

A wise guru had two disciples.

He gave each of his disciples a small sum of money and said, "Use this to go buy something that can completely fill this hut where I live."

One disciple went and bought a huge load of hay and with that hay he filled the hut.

"You disappoint me," said the guru, and he threw all the hay into the woods.

The other disciple used the money to buy a candle, and the candle filled every corner of the hut with light.

The guru smiled. "That," he said, "is the light of wisdom indeed."

148. THE BEGGAR AND EMPEROR AKBAR

A poor man came to beg from Emperor Akbar.

As he waited with the other petitioners, he heard the emperor praying. "O God, I pray that you grant me prosperity, I pray that you grant me…" and so on.

The beggar then got up to leave, which attracted the emperor's attention.

"Hey there!" shouted Emperor Akbar. "Why are you leaving? Didn't you come for something?"

"I did," the beggar replied. "But then I heard your prayer and realized you too are a beggar, just like me. If I must beg, then I will beg help from God, not from you."

149. THE WIDOW AND HER SONS

A widow lived with her sons and their wives who all treated her unkindly.

One day she wandered outside of town. She found an abandoned house in ruins and without a roof.

She went inside.

"My elder son treats me unkindly!" she said to one wall, venting her frustrations in detail; the wall collapsed.

She felt lighter!

Then she vented her frustration with her other son to another wall; it also collapsed.

Then she complained about her daughters-in-law to the two remaining walls. They collapsed.

Standing in the heap of rubble, she felt happy again, and ready to return home.

150. THE OLD WOMAN GOING TO TOWN

A young man riding horseback passed an old woman on the way to town.

"Poor thing!" he said as he rode by. "It's going to take you all day to get to town on those old legs."

"Hurry on your way, young man," she said. "I'll get there, God willing."

Along the way the young man talked to various friends, took a nap, and spent some time adjusting his turban to look especially elegant.

Imagine his surprise when he reached town and found the old woman already there.

"With my old legs," she said, smiling, "I have outpaced your horse."

151. THE COUPLE WHO COOPERATED

In a village there lived a woman who could not walk because she had lost the use of her legs. In that same village, there lived a man who could not see because he had lost the use of his eyes.

Floodwaters came, and all the villagers ran, abandoning these two to their fate in the rushing waters.

"Help me!" shouted the lame woman, and the blind man lifted her up on his shoulders.

"Help me!" shouted the blind man, and the lame woman told him which way to go.

Thus they escaped the floodwaters, working for each other's safety.

152. THE BLIND MEN AND THE ELEPHANT

A guide was leading four blind men through a jungle when they came upon an elephant.

One man felt the leg. "There's a pillar here!"

A second touched the trunk. "No, it's a mighty warrior's club!"

The third held the elephant's ear. "You're both wrong. This is a winnowing basket!"

The fourth rubbed the elephant's belly, laughing. "You fools! It's a big jar."

Then the guide explained to them, "This is an elephant: not a pillar or a club or a basket or a jar. You must explore all the parts, and then use your imagination to know the elephant."

153. THE BRAHMIN'S GOAT

A brahmin was carrying a goat to the temple.

Three bandits were hidden along his path; they wanted that goat.

"Why are you carrying a dog?" the first bandit shouted.

"No!" the brahmin retorted. "It's a goat." He kept on walking.

"Why are you carrying a calf?" the second bandit shouted.

"No!" the brahmin insisted. "It's a goat." He kept on walking.

"Why are you carrying a donkey?" the third bandit shouted.

The brahmin was now terrified. "It must be a shape-shifting demon!" he thought, dropping the goat and fleeing as fast as he could.

The bandits got the goat.

154. THE FARMER AND THE MERCHANT

A farmer left his plowshare with a merchant friend while he traveled.

"I'll keep it safe for you," the merchant promised.

When the farmer returned, the merchant explained that the farmer's plowshare had disappeared. "The mice must have eaten it," he said.

"Mice can't eat iron!" retorted the farmer, but the merchant swore it was true.

The farmer then kidnapped the merchant's son.

"Where's my son?" the merchant asked.

"An eagle carried him off."

"An eagle couldn't do that!"

"No more than mice can eat iron."

Thus the merchant returned the farmer's plowshare, and the farmer returned the merchant's son.

155. THE MONK AND THE KING

A monk came to the king. "I journey to heaven each night!" he boasted. Intrigued, the king invited the monk to stay in the royal guesthouse.

The next morning, the monk proclaimed, "I bring you greetings from the gods in heaven!"

The king's minister was not impressed, so that night he had wood heaped around the guesthouse.

"What are you doing?" asked the king.

"The monk's earthly body will burn," the minister said. "Then we'll see his heavenly body."

The guesthouse burned down, and no one saw the monk again.

"No doubt he stayed in heaven," thought the foolish king.

156. THE POTTER AND THE KING

A clumsy potter fell on some pots and cut his head, leaving a deep scar across his forehead.

When the king called for volunteer soldiers, the potter decided he'd prefer to be a soldier than a potter.

Seeing the scar, the king thought he must be a valiant warrior and made him a lieutenant.

Later, however, the army's general asked the potter how he got that scar.

"I fell down and cut my head," said the potter honestly.

The general laughed. "You better go home now," he said, "before you get hurt even more badly pretending to be a soldier."

157. THE CARPENTER AND HIS SON

There was once a foolish man, and he had a foolish son. The foolish man was a carpenter, and his son worked as his assistant.

One day the carpenter was working in his workshop when a mosquito landed on his head.

"Get rid of that mosquito for me, son," he said.

The son picked up an ax and he hit the mosquito.

"I got him!" shouted the son.

Alas, the blow of the ax also cut his father's head in two.

What is the moral of the carpenter's story?

The Buddha says: A foolish friend is worse than an enemy.

158. THE MAN IN THE TREE

A foolish man was stuck in a tree.

An elephant-driver riding an elephant came by. "I'll help you!" he said.

But when the elephant-driver reached up with his elephant-hook to grab the man in the tree, the elephant bolted.

Now the elephant-driver was dangling from the man in the tree.

"Let's sing loudly!" said the foolish man. "Someone will hear and come help."

The elephant-driver began to sing.

"Bravo! You're a good singer!" said the foolish man, and when he applauded, they both fell out of the tree and were killed.

If you want to help a fool, be careful.

159. THE MERCHANT AND HIS SERVANT

A silk-merchant was traveling to the market.

Along the way, the merchant's camel collapsed.

"I'll go buy a new camel," he told his servant. "You stay here, and make sure not to let my leather trunks get wet in the rain."

The merchant left.

Later, it rained.

The servant was desperate. "How will I keep the rain off the trunks?" he wondered.

Then he had an idea!

He took the bolts of silk out of the trunks and wrapped the silk around the trunks.

When the merchant returned, he was furious: the trunks were safe but the silk was ruined.

160. THE TWO BROTHERS

There were once two foolish brothers.

Their father died, and his will said:

Divide everything equally.

First, they divided the farm. "You take the west half; I'll take the east," said the one brother.

Then the house. "You take the top half; I'll take the bottom," said the other.

Then they cut each piece of furniture in the house in half.

Then they began cutting the livestock in half: chickens, goats, cows, everything.

Finally, they cut the servants in half.

The police then came and arrested the two brothers.

They were hanged for murder, and they divided the gibbet equally.

161. THE FIVE LOAVES OF BREAD

There was a very hungry man who bought five loaves of bread at the bakery.

First, he ate one loaf, but he was still hungry.

"That loaf didn't work," he thought. "Maybe the next one will!"

So he ate the second loaf, but he was still hungry.

Then he ate the third, and then the fourth.

None of them worked!

Finally, he ate the fifth loaf.

"Ah," he sighed, "at last my hunger is satisfied. I just wish I had known it was this particular loaf that I needed. I could have eaten this one first and saved the rest."

162. THE MAN AND HIS NEIGHBOR

A man came knocking on his neighbor's door in the middle of the night.

"Help me, neighbor!" he shouted.

"What is it?" said his neighbor sleepily as he opened the door. "What's wrong?"

"I wanted to smoke my pipe," said the man, "so I came here to ask you for a light."

"You aren't even paying attention!" groaned the neighbor. "You have woken me up to give you a light, but you have a lighted lantern right there in your hand."

The moral: The solution to a problem might be in your own hands, but you fail to see it.

163. THE JUDGE AND HIS SON

A farmer's wife was sleeping with the judge and with the judge's son.

One day, the son was there when his father arrived.

"Hide in the closet!" she said.

The judge came in.

Then she saw her husband coming too.

"Leave now, and look angry!" she told the judge.

"Why was the judge so angry?" her husband asked.

"He's angry at his son! I don't know why," she said. "The son needed to hide, so I put him in the closet. Come out now, boy! Your father's gone."

The judge's son thanked them both.

"You're welcome!" said the gullible husband.

164. THE WIFE WHO DIED

An unfaithful wife plotted with her maid.

"Tell my husband I'm dead!" she said.

The maid took the grieving husband to the burning-grounds and showed him someone else's remains.

Tearfully, he accepted the ashes and bones.

Then, he prepared his wife's funeral. The maid recommended the wife's lover as a worthy brahmin the husband could employ.

As the pretend-brahmin was conducting the ritual, the wife appeared and joined in the feast.

"How can this be?" exclaimed the husband, amazed that she could attend her own funeral.

"Your wife's great chastity," explained the maid, "allows her to enjoy the funeral feast."

165. THE CARPENTER UNDER THE BED

The carpenter suspected his wife was unfaithful, so he hid under the bed and waited.

The wife thought he was gone and invited her lover to come.

Then his wife heard him under the bed, so she screamed, "Hands off, villain!"

Her lover was confused.

"A goddess predicted my husband would die unless I brought a stranger into my bed," she said. "You're in; now get out!"

"Such devotion!" yelled the carpenter joyfully. "Thank you both!"

He then stood up under the bed, lifting the bed on his back, and carried the lovers on the bed all around the village.

166. TENALIRAMA AND KALI

Young Tenalirama prayed to Kali.

The goddess appeared to him, holding two bowls. "Choose!" she commanded. "The milk of learning or the curds of wealth."

"I'm not sure…" he replied.

The boy then snatched the two bowls and swallowed both milk and curds.

"O Kali Ma," he quickly explained, "there was no choosing; one without the other would be useless."

Kali frowned and then laughed. "You will pay a price for this disobedience! Though learned and prosperous, you will be laughed at: you'll be Tenalirama the jester."

Tenalirama bowed in reverence and gratitude.

When he looked up, she was gone.

167. TENALIRAMA AND THE KING

King Krishnadevaraya invited everyone in the city to a royal feast.

Young Tenalirama pushed his way to the front of the crowd to listen to the king's guru.

"What you see is only what you think you see," intoned the guru. "All differences are Maya, thought-illusion. Seeing, hearing, tasting: it is all in your mind."

Tenalirama laughed loudly.

"Why are you laughing, boy?" asked the king.

"I was just thinking that I'll gladly eat the guru's portion at the feast," Tenalirama replied. "I'll taste the food while he thinks about it."

The king laughed and made Tenalirama his royal jester.

168. TENALIRAMA AND THE GOLD COINS

Tenalirama was still new to the court, and he was surprised when King Krishnadevaraya unexpectedly gave him a gift of gold coins. Where to put the coins? He tried stuffing them into his pockets, but the fabric ripped and the coins spilled onto the floor.

As Tenalirama rushed to pick them up, the king's other courtiers all laughed.

"Don't be so miserly!" said the king. "That's undignified for a courtier."

"O Your Majesty, your likeness is on every coin, and you should not be lying on the dusty floor or trampled underfoot," Tenalirama explained. "That's undignified for a king."

169. TENALIRAMA AND THE PEACHES

The Emperor of China sent a gift of fruits no one had seen before: peaches. With the box was a note, which King Krishnadevaraya read aloud: "This food brings long life and happiness to whoever eats it."

Intrigued, Tenalirama reached out, took a peach and bit into it. "Delicious!" he said.

The king was outraged. "How dare you grab a peach without permission! To the dungeons! Off with his head!"

Tenalirama then shook the peach angrily. "It's a trap!" he shouted. "The peach doesn't grant long life; it has killed me!"

The king laughed, and then he shared the peaches.

170. TENALIRAMA AND THE TWENTY LASHES

King Krishnadevaraya was furious at Tenalirama. "Stay away! If I see you again, you'll get twenty lashes."

Tenalirama returned the next day.

"You're not allowed in!" said the outer guard.

"But the king promised me a present," said Tenalirama. "I'll give you half!"

Tenalirama then made the same deal with the inner guard.

When Tenalirama entered the court, the king yelled, "I warned you: twenty lashes!"

"Wait," said Tenalirama, and he summoned the guards.

"Ten lashes for him," said the jester, "and ten for him."

The king had to laugh at Tenalirama's ingenuity, and he even spared the greedy guards.

171. TENALIRAMA AND THE WASHERMAN

Enraged by Tenalirama's pranks, King Krishnadevaraya shouted, "Bury him up to his neck! Let an elephant trample his head!"

So the guards buried Tenalirama and went to fetch an elephant.

A washerman walked by, carrying a heavy laundry-basket. "Oh, my arthritis!" the washerman groaned.

"This cure works!' shouted Tenalirama. "I buried myself, and my arthritis is cured. Try it! I'll bury you, and I'll deliver the laundry!"

The washerman agreed.

Tenalirama buried him and ran off.

Then the washerman saw the elephant coming.

"HELP!" he yelled.

The guards stopped the elephant just in time.

Tenalirama had outwitted everyone once again.

172. TENALIRAMA AND THE EXECUTIONER

Tenalirama's latest prank infuriated King Krishnadevaraya.

"Take him away!" he said to the executioner. "Cut off his head with one slice of your sword!"

The executioner grabbed Tenalirama.

"Let me pray in the holy river first," the jester begged.

They waded into the river. Tenalirama prayed quietly and then yelled, "CUT!" The executioner swung his sword, but Tenalirama had plunged into the water. The sword whooshed through the air.

The executioner chased Tenalirama onto the bank and prepared to swing again.

"Stop!" Tenalirama yelled. "The king said 'one slice of your sword' — one only!"

So Tenalirama escaped punishment again.

173. TENALIRAMA AND HIS BROTHER-IN-LAW

Tenalirama's greedy brother-in-law raided the royal orchard, so King Krishnadevaraya ordered him to be executed.

Tenalirama's sister begged Tenalirama to help them, and he agreed to intercede with the king.

As soon as the king saw Tenalirama he shouted, "I know why you're here: it's to save that wretched brother-in-law of yours! Well, I absolutely refuse to do whatever you ask on his behalf. I won't do it!"

Tenalirama smiled. "I was coming here to ask you to execute him, rascal that he is. But I understand: you will not execute him."

The king laughed.

Tenalirama had done it again!

174. TENALIRAMA AND THE QUEEN

King Krishnadevaraya recited his poem for the queen, and she yawned.

"I'll never forgive you!" the king shouted.

The queen asked Tenalirama for help.

The next day, the king and his court discussed the drought afflicting the kingdom.

"I have a solution!" shouted Tenalirama, holding up a sack of seeds. "This wheat grows without any rain at all."

"Wonderful!" shouted the king happily.

"The only condition," Tenalirama said, "is that whoever plants the seed must have never yawned in his life. Not once. Ever."

The king was bewildered, but then he understood. "I will forgive the queen," he said, smiling.

175. TENALIRAMA'S FINGER

King Krishnadevaraya was extremely fastidious.

"I see dirt under that fingernail," he shouted at Tenalirama. "Cut that finger off!"

"I'll clean it carefully," replied Tenalirama.

"No! Cut it off!"

Tenalirama disappeared for a few days. He made a pit filled with mud and covered with turf ... exactly where the king liked to walk.

When the king fell into the mud up to his neck, Tenalirama appeared with a sword. "I'll cut right at the neck!" he shouted.

The king understood and laughed.

"Just get me out of here!" he said. "And you can forget what I said about the finger."

176. TENALIRAMA'S FACE

Tenalirama had done it again: King Krishnadevaraya was furious at his latest prank.

"Get out of here!" the king shouted at him. "And never show your face in court again!"

The next day, the king was shocked when the herald announced Tenalirama was coming. When the jester entered, the king saw he had a huge iron soup pot on his head.

"Greetings, Your Highness!" Tenalirama shouted, his words echoing weirdly inside the pot.

"But I told you…"

"You told me never to show my face in court again," said Tenalirama.

The king laughed and forgave Tenalirama, as he always did.

177. TENALIRAMA AND THE CHESSBOARD

Tenalirama's latest poem delighted King Krishnadevaraya.

"Name your reward!" the king proclaimed.

Tenalirama pointed to the king's chessboard. "Just put one sesame seed here," he said, "and then two seeds on this square; four seeds here; then eight, and so on. That will satisfy me!'

The king laughed. "That's too small a reward for such a great poem!"

"Not at all!" Tenalirama replied, smiling.

The king quickly discovered that Tenalirama was correct: it would bankrupt the whole treasury to cover the chessboard with sesame seeds that way. The whole world did not contain enough sesame!

Again, Tenalirama had delighted the king.

178. TENALIRAMA AND THE PAINTER

"This is the best portrait I've ever seen!" King Krishnadevaraya said to the royal painter. "I must reward you. I'll make you prime minister."

The result was a complete disaster. The royal painter knew nothing of statecraft.

"Help me, Tenalirama!" he said.

Tenalirama organized a feast. The king started to eat, but spat the food out. "This is disgusting!" he shouted. "Summon the cook!"

The cook came in.

"But you're the royal carpenter!" said the king.

Tenalirama laughed. "And making a carpenter cook is about as bad as making a painter prime minister!"

The king laughed.

Tenalirama was right, again.

179. TENALIRAMA AND THE CHINESE VASES

The Chinese ambassador sent King Krishnadevaraya four beautiful vases.

"Death to anyone who breaks a vase!' proclaimed the king.

A servant accidentally broke a vase and was sentenced to death.

Tenalirama visited him in prison.

At the execution, the servant begged, "Please, Your Highness, let me see the three remaining vases."

The king agreed.

When he saw the vases, the servant burst free and smashed them all.

"They would get broken eventually," he said. "I didn't want anyone else to have to die for it."

The king understood: people matter more than vases.

"Free the prisoner!" he said.

Tenalirama smiled.

180. TENALIRAMA AND THE KING'S BAD LUCK

King Krishnadevaraya had a servant nicknamed "Bad-Luck."

The first person who saw Bad-Luck's face first each day had bad luck all day long.

One early morning the king visited the kitchen; there he saw Bad-Luck, and then he had a terrible day: bad news, bad headache, everything bad.

"I'm going to execute that servant!" the king shouted.

As Tenalirama led Bad-Luck to the gallows, he said, "O King, consider this: you saw Bad-Luck's face first today, and he saw yours first. Now he's facing death. Whose face is more unlucky?"

The king laughed. "Release the prisoner!"

Tenalirama had triumphed again.

181. TENALIRAMA AND THE MAGICIAN

A magician arrived, boasting of powers greater than any member of King Krishnadevaraya's court.

"You must defeat him, Tenalirama!" begged the king.

Tenalirama confronted the magician. "You cannot do with your eyes open what I can do with my eyes shut!" the jester proclaimed.

"Of course I can!" countered the magician.

Tenalirama took a sack of chili-powder, shut his eyes, and put chili-powder on both eyelids. He then counted to one hundred, smiling.

Next, Tenalirama washed the powder off carefully and handed the sack to the magician.

The magician ran away without so much as a word.

Tenalirama had won!

182. TENALIRAMA'S RAMAYANA

A courtesan invited Tenalirama to recite the Ramayana, the epic story of Rama's adventures, just for her.

Tenalirama began with the story of King Dasharatha and Rama's birth, followed by the intrigue in King Dasharatha's court, then Rama's exile into the forest, accompanied by his devoted wife Sita and his loyal brother Lakshmana.

"So," he said, "Rama, accompanied by Sita and Lakshmana, went into the forest to begin their exile."

Then Tenalirama fell silent.

The courtesan waited, and finally she could wait no longer. "Then what happened?" she demanded.

"Be patient," said Tenalirama. "They are still walking through the forest."

183. TENALIRAMA AND THE RAMAYANA MURALS

The royal painter decorated the palace walls with Ramayana murals. Tenalirama scoffed. "Where's the rest of Lakshmana?" he asked, pointing to one figure.

"That's a profile!" replied the painter. "You have to imagine the rest."

"I will decorate the summer palace with my own Ramayana paintings!" boasted Tenalirama.

A month later, he was done. The king came to see ... and there were only noses. Everywhere! Noses painted all over the walls!

"What is this?" he shouted angrily.

"Well, this is Rama, of course. And Sita, Lakshmana..." Tenalirama pointed out each nose one by one. "You have to imagine the rest."

184. TENALIRAMA AND THE MONEY-BAG

Tenalirama was traveling home after a long journey.

It began to rain, so he sought refuge at an inn, hoping to dry himself by the fire. Unfortunately, there were others there already, and he couldn't even get close to the fire.

"Alas!" he shouted. "I've lost the royal money-bag! I must have dropped it when my horse slipped in the mud about a mile down the road. The king will be very angry!"

Everyone in the inn rushed out the door, hoping to find the lost money-bag.

Which did not exist, of course.

Meanwhile, Tenalirama dried himself by the fire.

185. TENALIRAMA AND THE THIEF

Tenalirama was on a journey, and a sadhu he met along the way asked to travel with him.

Tenalirama agreed, although he knew the man was not a saint; he was a thief who wanted to steal Tenalirama's money.

Every night, the thief would rummage through Tenalirama's bags and clothing, looking for the money, but he could never find where Tenalirama had hidden it.

When they reached their destination, he said, "I confess: I'm a thief, and you baffled me. Where did you hide your money?"

"I put it under your pillow," replied Tenalirama. "I knew you'd never look there."

186. TENALIRAMA AND THE HONEST BEGGAR

A beggar and a merchant came to Tenalirama for judgment.

"I saw he dropped this purse containing a hundred gold coins," said the beggar, "so I returned it to him."

"My purse contained two hundred gold coins," protested the merchant. "That thieving beggar owes me a hundred more!"

"I'm sure you both speak the truth," Tenalirama said, though he knew the merchant was a notorious liar.

"Keep the purse and coins," he told the beggar. "Nobody has reported a lost purse containing a hundred coins."

Then, he said to the merchant, smiling, "I hope someone finds your lost purse soon!"

187. TENALIRAMA AND THE CHICKEN

"I demand justice!" the farmer shouted. "That man's cart ran over my chicken! I demand a thousand coins!"

"A chicken's only worth four coins!" the driver insisted.

"But that chicken would have laid hundreds of eggs. You haven't killed one chicken: you've killed hundreds!"

"That also means hundreds of chickens you don't have to feed," said Tenalirama. "One chicken eats fifty pounds of grain yearly, so hundreds of chickens..." Tenalirama calculated silently. "This man owes you a thousand coins for lost chickens, and you owe him seven tons of saved grain."

"I'll take the four coins," said the farmer quickly.

188. TENALIRAMA AND THE SADHU

Tenalirama had heard of a new sadhu who was attracting crowds of worshipers. He went to see the would-be saint and was appalled. The man had no knowledge of sacred mantras; instead, he was reciting random gibberish.

"O Great Soul!" shouted Tenalirama as he approached the sadhu. "O Most Holy One!" He then reached out and plucked a hair from the sadhu's beard. "A single strand of hair from your beard will bless me forever!"

The crowd then rushed forward, everyone wanting to grab a hair from the sadhu's beard.

Terrified, the sadhu ran off, never to be seen again.

189. TENALIRAMA AND THE BOYS

Tenalirama couldn't concentrate; some boys playing ball outside his house were making too much noise.

"How delightful!" he said. "You bring back memories of childhood! I'll pay you three silver coins each week to play here."

He paid them, and the boys were thrilled.

The next week, he paid just two coins. "I'm short on cash!"

The week after, he paid only one coin. "My own master hasn't paid me."

The third week, he paid nothing. "But I'll do my best to pay you next week if I can."

The angry boys deserted his street and never came back.

Success!

190. TENALIRAMA AND HIS FRIEND

"My house is too small!" complained Tenalirama's friend.

"I can help you," Tenalirama promised. "But you must do exactly what I tell you."

"Agreed!" said his friend.

Tenalirama then told him to bring the cow, the pig, the goat, and all the chickens into the house, and to come back in a week.

A week later, his friend returned. "That made things worse, not better!" he moaned.

"Of course it did," said Tenalirama. "Now, put all the animals back out where they belong."

The friend came back smiling.

"Thank you, Tenalirama!" he said. "My house is so much bigger now!"

191. TENALIRAMA'S MAGICAL WATER

A friend of Tenalirama's wife came to him for help.

"I keep quarreling with my mother-in-law!" she said. "The things she says make me so angry."

Tenalirama smiled. "I will give you some magical water," he said, handing her a small bottle. "Before you reply to your mother-in-law, take a mouthful, close your eyes, count to three, then swallow. The magical water will help you!"

The woman returned a week later. "It's wonderful!" she said. "But I need more magical water."

Tenalirama laughed. "It's just regular water," he said. "The magic is in stopping yourself before you reply in anger."

192. BIRBAL'S HOUSE

A man rushing down the street ran right into Birbal.

"Excuse me!" he said. "Which is Birbal's house?"

"That one," Birbal replied, pointing to a house at the end of the street.

The man went running toward the house.

When Birbal arrived, the man was still banging on the door.

"Can I help you?" Birbal asked.

The man turned, surprised to see him again. "I have an urgent message for Birbal, but he isn't home."

"I'm Birbal!"

"Why didn't you say so?"

"You didn't ask," Birbal replied. "You need to ask the question for which you really want the answer!"

193. BIRBAL AND THE EGGPLANTS

"These eggplants are exquisite!" Emperor Akbar proclaimed one night at dinner.

"I agree, Your Highness," said Birbal.

"Perhaps you can compose an 'Ode to Eggplants' and sing their praises."

Birbal improvised the ode on the spot, and the emperor was delighted.

The imperial chef heard about this and served eggplant every evening with dinner.

A week later, Akbar groaned. "I'm sick of eggplants. Eggplants are disgusting."

"I agree, Your Highness," said Birbal.

"But you were singing their praises last week!" said the emperor.

"That's true, Your Highness," replied Birbal. "I am the servant of the emperor, not of the eggplants."

194. BIRBAL AND THE TWO MOTHERS

Two women brought a dispute to Akbar's court, and Akbar told Birbal to decide the case.

"This baby's mine!" shouted one woman.

"No, he's mine!" shouted the other.

"Bring a glass of poisoned milk," commanded Birbal.

He then gave the milk to the woman holding the baby. "Have the baby drink this, or drink it yourself."

She hesitated, but then tilted the milk into the baby's mouth.

The other woman screamed, grabbed the glass of milk, and drank the poison herself.

Birbal smiled. "The milk is not poisoned," he said gently. "And now I know the baby is indeed yours."

195. BIRBAL AND THE BEGGAR

A beggar inhaled the smell wafting from a kebab-shop.

"You must pay me for the smell!" shouted the shop owner.

"I have no money," protested the beggar, so the owner took him to Akbar's court, where Birbal was judge.

Birbal listened to both men's stories. Then he drew forth several coins from his own purse.

"Are you listening?" he said to the shop owner.

The man nodded eagerly, thinking Birbal was going to pay him.

Birbal then shook the coins in his cupped hands. "The sound of the coins is your payment for the smell of the food. Case dismissed!"

196. BIRBAL'S MAGICAL STICKS

Someone was robbing the imperial kitchen, but the steward didn't know who. "Help me, Birbal!" he pleaded.

Birbal gathered some sticks and then addressed the kitchen staff. "These are my magical detecting sticks; each is the same length." He gave each person a stick. "Put this under your pillow tonight. The thief's greedy thoughts will make his stick grow longer."

The next morning, the staff presented their sticks.

One stick was much shorter than the rest!

"Behold the thief, who cut his stick to make it shorter," proclaimed Birbal. "By trying to prove his innocence, he has revealed his guilt."

197. BIRBAL AND THE CROWS

"Birbal has the answer to every question!" boasted Emperor Akbar.

This made the other courtiers jealous.

One courtier decided to challenge Birbal. "Dear Birbal," he said, "please tell us how many crows live here in Agra."

Birbal answered instantly. "Eighty-nine thousand three hundred and twelve."

The courtier scoffed. "Suppose I count and find out that's too high?"

Birbal smiled. "It just means some crows are visiting their relatives in other cities. Of course, if you find more, some of those crows are visiting here from other cities; they don't actually live here."

The emperor laughed, delighted with Birbal as always.

198. THE EMPEROR'S CARAVANSARY

Strolling through the garden, Emperor Akbar and Birbal met a sadhu.

"How did you get here?" the emperor asked.

"How did you?" replied the sadhu.

"This is my palace!" exclaimed the emperor.

"I see no palace," replied the sadhu, "only a caravansary."

The emperor was speechless with rage.

"Tell me," said the sadhu, "who lived here before you?"

"My father."

"And before him?"

"His father."

"Guests come; guests go. You see: only a caravansary."

The emperor smiled. "A good lesson. What may I give you in return?"

"Just move along," said the sadhu. "You're blocking the sun that warms me."

199. BIRBAL SEES BOTH GOOD AND BAD

A fellow courtier complained, "My prize Arabian mare ran away!"

"That could be good," said Birbal, angering the courtier.

Then the mare returned, followed by a wild stallion.

"What wonderful good luck!" exclaimed the courtier.

"Though it could be bad," said Birbal, angering the courtier again.

The stallion then threw the courtier's son, breaking his leg.

"My poor boy!" sobbed the courtier.

"That could be very good," said Birbal.

"You're heartless!" the courtier replied, angrier than ever.

The next day, soldiers came to recruit able-bodied young men for the war; they did not take the courtier's son.

Birbal just smiled.

200. BIRBAL THE PHILOSOPHER

The emperor was feeling philosophical one evening.

"Why doesn't God just put a stop to evil?" he asked Birbal. "When I want something to top, I make it stop. God could use his powers to put a stop to all evil."

"That isn't how God created us," replied Birbal. "We are each a mix of good and evil, every one of us."

The emperor nodded thoughtfully.

"So," Birbal concluded, "if God were to rid the world of evil, he'd have to get rid of me and get rid of you too."

The emperor smiled, delighted as always by Birbal's wisdom.

Story Title Index

Story Sources

For story-specific bibliography and notes, visit:
India.LauraGibbs.net

Chalmers, Robert (translator). *The Jataka*.

Cowell, E. B. and W. H. D. Rouse (translators). *The Jataka*.

Dutton, Maude Barrows. *The Tortoise and the Geese, and Other Fables of Bidpai*.

Francis, H.T. and R.A. Neil (translators). *The Jataka*.

Goyal, Vishal. *Fix Your Problems the Tenali Raman Way*.

Hale-Wortham, B. (translator). *Hitopadesha, or, The Book of Good Counsel*.

Mandana, Kavitha. *Tenali Raman: Tales of Wit and Wisdom*.

Moseley, James. *A Caravan from Hindustan: The Complete Birbal Tales*.

Prasadh, Nagaraj. *Stories of Lord Ganesha.*

Raju, Ramaswami. *Indian Fables.*

Ramakrishna. *Tales and Parables.*

Ramanujan, A. K. *Folktales from India.*

Rangachari, Devika. *The Wit of Tenali Raman.*

Rouse, W.H.D. (translator). *The Jataka.*

Ryder, Arthur (translator). *The Panchatantra.*

Steel, Flora Annie. *Tales of the Punjab.*

Tawney, C.H. (translator). *The Ocean of Story.*

Venkataswami, M. N. *Heeramma and Venkataswami, or Folktales From India.*

Venkataswami, M. N. *Tulsemmah and Nagaya.*

Printed in Great Britain
by Amazon